Finding Hope
A Rescue Alaska Mystery

by

Kathi Daley

Chapter 1

With eighteen hours of sunlight in August, the days are long in Rescue, which I guessed helped to equal out the short days experienced in December when dark skies made up twenty-one of the twenty-four hours in any given day. As a lifelong resident of this Northern Alaska town, I'm used to both the abnormally long and short days. But with a full-time job, volunteer duties at the local animal shelter, and six dogs, four cats, eight rabbits, and a blind mule to take care of, if given a choice, I supposed I'd take the long days over the short ones.

Of course, my role as a member of Rescue, Alaska's search and rescue team generally became more demanding during the summer when groups from the lower forty-eight descended on the area for an outback adventure. I tried to be mentally prepared for last-minute disruptions in my everyday life, but on this particular day, the call came early. Really, really early.

"Hello," I said, my voice still groggy with sleep.

"Harmony, it's Jake." Jake Cartwright was my best friend and brother-in-law. My only family since my sister, Val, died during the execution of a rescue when I was seventeen.

"I'm assuming, due to the god-awful hour of your call, that we have a rescue."

"We do," Jake confirmed. "Eight teens from Fairbanks headed out on a backpacking trip nine days ago. They were due to return in seven days. None have been seen or heard from since they left. I realize that it's possible the group simply became distracted and lost track of the number of days they'd been away, but the parents of these eight teens have organized and are demanding that we look for them."

"Houston?" I asked about Police Chief Hank Houston of Rescue, Alaska's police force.

"He's on his way over. I'm not sure if this will turn out to be a police matter, but he offered to help, and I'm inclined to let him. Landon and Wyatt are on their way as well." Landon Stanford and Wyatt Forrester were longtime members of the team. "We're hoping to head out within the hour. Can you get here?"

I thought about the animals I needed to feed and let out. "I'll try. I'm getting up now. I have to see to the animals, so I doubt I can make it in an hour, but I'll hurry."

"Just get here when you can."

Rolling out of bed, I began to dress in layers. At this time of the year, temperatures up on the mountain can vary by as much as forty degrees in a single twenty-four-hour period. I decided to let the dogs out to run while I attended to the animals in the barn. Usually, I liked to take the dogs for a nice long hike in the mornings, but there simply wouldn't be time this morning. Perhaps I'd call my good friend, Harley Medford, and ask him if he would be willing to stop by and take the dogs for a stroll down to the lake this afternoon. Harley was an actor with a successful career who spent half his time in Los Angeles and the other half here in Rescue. He had a dog named Brando who came over to play with my pack on a regular basis, so all my dogs, even my very protective wolf hybrid, Denali, should be fine with his presence in the event I couldn't make it home in a reasonable amount of time.

Once I'd fed the animals that lived in the barn, I called the dogs in and fed them. Next came the cats, and once they were settled, I washed up a bit, called my search and rescue dog, Yukon, grabbed my backpack and rifle, and Yukon and I headed out for what I hoped would be an uncomplicated rescue. In my experience, while the vast majority of the rescues we were called out on worked out just fine, the rescues after an exceptionally harsh winter and late thaw led to the most dangerous situations. The runoff caused by melting snow generally means avalanches, dangerously full rivers, and unstable glaciers that could give way if an inexperienced or uninformed hiker attempted to cross them.

By the time I arrived at Neverland, the bar owned by Jake, which doubled as the headquarters for our search and rescue team, the other members of the team had already arrived. Jake handed me a photo of the group who were missing that had been posted on social media as the friends prepared to head out for their hike. Once everyone had been given a chance to study the photo, he jumped into his overview.

"Eight teenagers, four boys and four girls, left for a backpacking trip nine days ago. They were due to return to Fairbanks two days ago but never showed up," Jake began. "The photo I have passed out was taken as the group prepared to set out. We assume that someone the group met at the trailhead shot the photo, but at this point, we don't know who snapped it. We do know that the photo was posted to Brit Johnson's social media accounts just as the group prepared to enter the wilderness area. Brit is the dark-haired girl with the green sweatshirt in the center. She's seventeen years old, a high school senior, and a long-distance runner. I spoke to her mother, who informed me that while Brit has limited experience backpacking, she's spent considerable time running on her own and is both cautious and resourceful.

"I remember reading about her," Wyatt said. "She completed a hundred-mile run this past spring."

"A hundred miles all at once?" I asked as my mind refused to consider such a possibility.

"A hundred miles all at once," Wyatt confirmed. "Well, at least a hundred miles over the course of a day or perhaps a weekend. I'm sure the athletes have to stop to fuel and rehydrate."

"I remember reading that the athletes run the hundred-mile races in around thirteen hours," Dani Mathews, our helicopter pilot, said. "I'm sure some do it quicker, while others take longer, but it's still an amazing feat."

"I like to think that I'm in decent shape, but I'm pretty sure I couldn't run a hundred miles if my life depended on it," I added.

"If your life depended on it, you'd be able to go further than you might think," Wyatt said.

"Who's the boy with the blond hair and blue shirt standing next to Brit?" I asked.

"He looks familiar," Landon jumped in.

"His name is Braydon Justice," Jake provided. "He's eighteen and graduated from high school this past June. He was the star quarterback for his team in Fairbanks."

"I recognize the name. Braydon scored a scholarship to UCLA," Landon shared. "I read about him in the newspaper. There was a feature about how he underwent a series of surgeries to repair damage caused by a hereditary heart defect so he'd be eligible to play. He's a real success story."

"Getting into UCLA on a football scholarship is no easy feat," I agreed. "Who is the girl standing next to him?"

Jake answered. "The girl with the red hair standing to Braydon's left is Carrie Preston. She's the youngest at sixteen, is in advanced placement classes, and will be a high school senior next year. She's also the current girlfriend of Carter Harding, the boy to her left. Seventeen-year-old Carter will also be a senior next year."

"And the boy to Brit's right?" I asked.

"Pete Pinewood. He graduated with Braydon and is planning to attend Cal Poly in the fall. The girl next to him is Talia Thomas. She's the only teen who doesn't live in Fairbanks and is the cousin of Logan Burge, the tall boy standing to her right."

"And where does Talia live?" I asked.

"San Francisco," Jake answered. "From what I was able to gather, Logan and his family moved to Alaska from San Francisco a few years ago."

"And the girl standing to Logan's right?" I asked.

"The girl to Logan's right is Alice Covington. Alice is Logan's girlfriend, who I believe is also seventeen. I know Alice currently lives in Fairbanks, but it seems to me that she recently moved to Alaska. I believe she may be from Portland originally, but I'm not a hundred percent sure about that."

"I think what's important in all of this is that we find these teens," Dani said. "I guess having a background is important to a point, but I feel like we're wasting time going over so many details."

"I agree," Wyatt said. "We need to hit the trail and find these teens before something happens to them."

"Given the way this whole thing unfolded, I assume we don't have anything with a scent to follow," I stated.

"The vehicles the teens arrived in are still parked at the trailhead," Jake answered. "It's been over a week since they were in the vehicles, and there will be a lot of different scents for the dogs to sort through, but I thought we'd go ahead and expose the dogs to the car interiors all the same."

"How do you plan to execute the rescue?" Hank, who'd been listening quietly to this point, asked.

Jake responded. "I'll take Sitka and follow the marked trail that the backpackers would likely have taken when they left the parking area. You and Kojak can take the trail to the north, which parallels the main trail, and Harmony and Yukon can take the trail to the south, which parallels the main trail. Landon will go with Harmony, and Wyatt will go with you. Dani will head up for a birdseye view."

"And Jordan?" Dani asked. "Will she be joining us?"

"Jordan is on call should we need her," Jake informed the group. Jordan Fairchild was Jake's girlfriend, a doctor, and a search and rescue volunteer. "As always, Sarge will be manning the radio and making any corrections that are needed as we progress. Any other questions before we head out?"

No one had any questions, so everyone other than Dani, who headed toward the airport, headed toward the vehicles that would take us to the parking area where the eight backpackers had entered the wilderness area. Jake wanted me to try to psychically connect with one of the teens, which is an ability that I consider both a gift and a curse, so he suggested that Yukon and I drive to the trailhead with him and Sitka in his truck. Wyatt and Landon rode along with Houston and Kojak.

"Are you getting anything?" Jake asked as we sped along the deserted highway.

I'd closed my eyes and had been focusing in on each of the eight teens, one at a time. "No. I might do better having just one teen to focus on." I opened my eyes and looked at the photo. In order for me to connect, the individual I hoped to merge with psychically needed to be both alive and conscious. The individual also needed to be in a heightened state of awareness. In the beginning, I was only able to connect with those who were either terrified or in a great deal of pain, but my gift seemed to have grown, and recently, I'd been able to connect with select individuals I'd chosen who weren't necessarily under distress. "While any one of the teens could be injured and therefore susceptible to my ability to home in on them due to their pain, it seems more likely that one of the girls, perhaps Talia, who doesn't live in the area, would be frightened enough for me to pick up on."

I closed my eyes and pictured the girl. I tried to "see" her in my mind. After ten minutes without success, I decided to move on to Alice. Alice, with the pretty blond hair and bright blue eyes, had only recently moved to Alaska, so I expected that the experience of being lost in the Alaskan wilderness might be frightening enough for me to pick up on.

"Any luck?" Jake asked.

I could feel his impatience, which wasn't helping.

"No. I'm not getting anything. Are you sure these teens are lost? Maybe they were just having a good time and chose not to return when they'd arranged to."

"I suppose that's a real possibility. All the teens, other than Carrie, are either seventeen or eighteen. I suspect they are used to making their own decisions rather than checking in with their parents over every little thing." He took a breath as he turned from the highway onto the groomed dirt road that led to the parking area and trailhead. "The thing is that unless these teens turn up or find a way to contact someone outside the group, all we can do is consider them as missing and look for them."

I knew Jake was right, but it seemed odd that no one was coming through. "I tried and failed to connect with both Talia and Alice. I'll try either Carrie or Brit when we take a break."

"If the teens are in trouble, I wouldn't discount the fear the guys might experience just because they're guys," Jake said. "Maybe try Logan. He has his cousin and his girlfriend with him, and I'd be willing to bet that he feels responsible for both of them. If the group is in trouble, chances are he's feeling the stress of the whole thing."

"Okay. Do you want me to do it now or when we take a break?"

Jake parked the truck and prepared to exit the vehicle. "Take ten minutes to try while we expose the dogs to the cars, and then if you don't get anything, you can try again when we take a break, providing, of course, that we don't find the group in the meantime."

I got out of the truck, looked around for a quiet place to work, and then sat down on a rock. Once I was settled, I closed my eyes. Jake had taken Yukon with him, so I didn't have him to keep an eye on. Since Jake suggested I start with Logan, I pictured the teen in my mind. While I hadn't been able to make the sort of connection I usually did, I was able to pick up a glimmer of something. What that something was, I couldn't be sure, but at least I felt that I'd gotten closer than I had with the others I'd tried to connect with.

"Anything I can do to help?" Houston asked as he sat down beside me.

I opened my eyes. "Where's Kojak?"

"Jake has all three dogs and is feeding them scents. He asked me to let you know that we'll be ready to head out in a couple minutes."

"I feel like I got close to a connection with Logan but not close enough to provide any sort of help in terms of narrowing down a location. I'm not sure why the signal was so weak. To be honest, I'm not even sure it was Logan I came close to connecting with. It may have been one of the others who simply piggybacked onto my intention."

"How's your head?" he asked.

Houston knew better than most how intentionally trying to mentally merge with the victims I was trying to connect with messed with my head, causing severe headaches I could barely tolerate at times.

"I'm okay. I think I'm actually getting better at making a connection without the pain. It's almost like my ability is a muscle I've been working and developing."

He stood up, took my hand in his, and pulled me to my feet. "I'm happy to hear that. I've always hated to see you in so much pain."

Houston and I had a long and complicated relationship. He'd been with me through good times and bad, and he'd been one of my chief supporters when it came to my gift and the evolution of that gift. Initially, all I'd been able to muster was a one-way link to victims I was meant to help rescue, but lately, my abilities had developed into much more.

"Are you still having the nightmares?" he asked.

"No, not since the kidnapping."

Two months ago, my gift had caused Houston to become a victim rather than a rescuer due to his proximity to me. He'd been seriously injured, but in the weeks after the incident, his body had healed, and it seemed that his mind had found peace as well. Of course, even though Houston was better, I still found it hard to forgive myself for the part I'd played in his near death. When he'd taken some time away from Alaska immediately following the ordeal, I'd been afraid that he wouldn't return, and if he had chosen to leave the tiny town where I'd lived my entire life, I wouldn't have blamed him. But a few weeks ago, Houston showed up at Neverland looking healthy and tanned. By all appearances, it seemed like he'd picked up right where he'd left off.

"Have you connected at all since then?" he wondered.

I shook my head. "No. I guess not." I looked him in the eye. "The experience we went through was intense. I think that subconsciously, or maybe even consciously, I've been avoiding anything that might cause a repeat." I took a breath. "Don't tell Jake this, but when he called and asked me to help today, the first thing I felt was terror. But then I thought about it and realized that these teens might really be in trouble, and if I could help, then I needed to try to do so."

He squeezed my hand. "I understand how you feel. It took me a while to get over all the conflicting emotions I needed to sort through after our adventure. But I think I'm mostly past it. Sometimes all you can do is force yourself to forge ahead."

I gave Houston a hug as Jake walked up with all three dogs.

"I guess we're ready," he said. "Any luck?"

"Not really," I answered and then shared with him the experience that I'd had.

"Okay, then we'll head out according to the plan. Make sure your radio is on channel two. The less accessed trails your team and Houston's team are going to head out on remain parallel to the main trail for the first couple of miles. About three miles in, the trail to the left heads up to Sequin Lake. If we haven't found the teens or at least picked up their trail at that point, I guess we'll need to discuss a strategy, but I'm thinking that unless we find evidence to suggest that the teens didn't stick to their plan, we'll all change course and meet up at Glacier Lake."

"Do we know where the teens were headed after Glacier Lake?" I asked Jake.

"The worried mother I spoke to said that Brit told her they were heading to Glacier Lake for three nights, then they planned to camp at Aloha Lake for two nights, and then circle around and hit Sapphire Lake on the way out. My plan is for us to make the loop, keeping our eyes open for places where the teen's plan may have deviated along the way."

The loop Jake described was about fifteen miles from start to finish. Doable in a day without heavy backpacks containing camping equipment as long as the weather held, which, based on the sunny sky overhead, it appeared that it just might.

"It doesn't look as if anyone has accessed this trail since the last rain," Landon said after the larger group had broken up and everyone headed down the paths assigned to them. While we were spread out a little bit, we were all headed toward Glacier Lake, the first lake the group planned to stop and camp at.

"The trail is tellingly free of footprints," I agreed. "The reality is that the group likely accessed Glacier Lake via the trail Jake is walking, but I understand why he thought it might be beneficial to spread out a bit. At least in the beginning."

"The snowmelt was late this year. There likely haven't been a lot of campers up this way. Maybe day hikers, but with the nighttime temperatures, I doubt there have been a lot of folks looking for an overnight adventure."

I glanced at Yukon, who was walking ahead of us but hadn't once alerted he'd found anything. "I wonder why this particular group came all the way up here if they wanted to go camping. I would understand if a group of seasoned backpackers wanted to make the trip, but it seems to me that a group of teens would be more likely to head to the beach for a post-graduation celebration."

Landon picked up a colorful rock, looked it over closely, and then tossed it away. "Chances are a single teen had an interest in a backcountry trip and convinced the others. It is nice and quiet up here. The daytime temperatures have been close to perfect for strenuous hiking, and while the nights have been cold, they haven't been so cold that a good night's sleep wouldn't be possible with a heavy-duty sleeping bag and a sturdy tent."

"I guess that's true. I've camped up here myself in the past, and it is nice and quiet."

"Did you come alone?" Landon asked.

"No, not alone. I came a few times with Jake and Val before she died, and I've been once or twice with just Jake since then. I dated this guy from Canada for a while, and we spent two weeks up here in late May one year."

"Late May sounds cold."

"It was, but I have arctic gear, and so did he. It was actually kind of romantic. In a way, it felt like we were the only two people on earth."

"I haven't personally been up here that early in the season, but if you don't mind trudging through snow that has yet to melt and have access to really good equipment, I can see how being up here all alone would be nice. Dangerous for the novice backpacker, but nice all the same."

"There can be a problem with avalanches at this time of the year." I agreed. "I remember this one rescue the team went out on the spring before Val died," I began.

"Jake to the rescue crew," Jake said over the radio, interrupting our conversation.

"Harmony, Yukon, and Landon here," I responded.

"Sitka and I are approaching the trail that heads up to Glacier Lake. Have you found any evidence that the group took either parallel trail or headed off in a different direction than the itinerary provided to me by Brit's mother?"

Houston and I each reported that our teams hadn't found any indication that anyone had accessed the less-used parallel trails in recent weeks.

"Okay, then let's all meet up at Glacier Lake. If the teens stopped and camped there, the dogs might be able to pick up a scent even if they've since moved on. I'm heading up now and should be there in about twenty minutes."

"We're right behind you," I said.

"Yeah, us as well," Houston parroted.

I glanced at Landon. "I have a bad feeling about things."

"A bad feeling?" he asked. "Do you sense something specific?"

I paused and then answered. "No, not really. It's just a gut instinct that seems to be telling me that all is not well with the group as we all hoped."

"Then I guess we'd better pick up the pace."

I agreed, and we headed out slightly faster than we'd been walking. By the time Landon, Yukon, and I arrived at Glacier Lake, Houston, Kojak, and Wyatt had joined Jake and Sitka.

"Oh my," I said, coming to a complete standstill. "What happened here?"

"I'm not sure," Jake said. "But based on the look of things, I'm going to go out on a limb and say that it wasn't anything good."

Chapter 2

"It looks like a grizzly bear came through here," Wyatt said as we all looked around the campsite in horror. There was a tent that had been ripped to shreds, discarded cookware, random clothing strewn around the area, and at least one backpack that had been emptied and discarded.

"Not a grizzly bear," Houston said as he slid a finger into the torn opening that had been created in the tent that had been left behind.

"You think *someone* rather than *something* did this," I stated.

Houston nodded. "I'd be willing to bet this tear was made by a knife, not a claw."

"Houston's right," Jake said, slipping his backpack off and setting it on a rock. "Based on all the footprints, I'm going to say a struggle of some sort between two or more humans is responsible for this mess."

"I'd say we should call the police, but the police are already here," Wyatt said, looking at Houston.

"What do you want us to do?" I asked.

"I'm going to see if I can get someone up here to process this campsite." He looked around. "It doesn't appear that anyone is still here, but perhaps you should look around while I make my call. If a person did this, then it seems likely that those teens aren't just off messing around as we all hoped they were."

"I had the same feeling while we were hiking up here," I confirmed.

"Let's divide up and each walk half a mile in a different direction, carefully looking for clues along the way," Jake instructed. "If you find something that looks like a clue, call me on the radio. If you don't find anything, come back to the campsite once you've traveled half a mile."

The four of us, with the three dogs, set off in different directions. Houston didn't need Kojak to make his call, so he'd instructed his dog to go with Wyatt. Landon was actually the one who picked up the trail, and while the news wasn't great, it did appear that there were nine separate sets of footprints within the perimeter of the campsite.

"Eight teens, nine sets of footprints," Jake said. "Someone was up here with them."

"Assuming that our search for these teens is going to be more difficult than just walking a loop in a single day, we're going to need supplies," I said. "Walking the fifteen miles in one day was doable as long as we kept going, but if we are going to need to stop to gather evidence left in the area, there really isn't any way to tell how long we might be out here." I frowned. "I will also need to make arrangements for my animals."

"Dani can bring supplies," Jake suggested. "There's a place where she can land on the other side of the lake."

"With the long days, the drop in temperature shouldn't be a problem as long as we have what we need to make a fire and maybe a couple sturdy tents and sleeping bags all around," Landon added.

Jake looked at me. "Can you call Chloe or maybe Serena and have them take care of your menagerie?"

"I'll make some calls," I said. Both friends had taken care of my animals in the past, and they knew what to do. "Speaking of calls, has anyone tried to track the cell phones these teens likely brought with them?"

"There's no cell service out here," Landon informed me. "You have a satellite phone." He looked around at the group. "We all do, but it is likely those teens had regular cell phones."

"Even Brit?" I asked. "It seems that if I was the sort of person to head off alone on hundred-mile runs, I'd want a portable phone that wasn't dependent on a nearby cell tower."

"Good point," Jake said. "I'll call Dani and let her know what we're going to need. Houston is on the phone with his office, trying to get help. You can use this time to call someone to take care of your animals, and Landon can call Brit's mother and try to find out exactly what sort of phone setup she has."

"What about me?" Wyatt asked Jake.

"Start looking around. Look for anything that might provide a clue as to what happened here."

It took a couple hours for our group to arrange what needed to be arranged. Dani agreed to bring the supplies we'd need to survive being out in the elements overnight. Since no one was currently available to process the campsite, Houston's assistant agreed to deliver an evidence kit to Dani, which he would use to collect and process any evidence he thought might be relevant. I spoke with Harley, who assured me that between him and Serena, they'd make sure my "kids" were fed, watered, and walked and that their environments were cleaned.

With all of that arranged, it was time to develop a plan. Landon had a long conversation with Brit's mother, who was surprisingly calm given the situation. She informed him that Brit had both a standard cell phone and an expensive satellite phone and that she'd been trying to reach Brit via both phones with no luck so far. We supposed it was likely that if a person was responsible for what had occurred at the campsite, then that person may have noticed Brit's cell phone and taken it or, at the very least, disabled it.

"With the long day of sunlight, we can easily make it to the second campsite on the list provided by Brit's mother," Wyatt said. "It seems as if we should keep moving even if we need to move at a slower pace."

"Once Dani gets here with the supplies, we'll move on," Jake agreed.

"I'll need an hour with my evidence kit," Houston informed us.

"I know how to get to Aloha Lake," Landon said. "I'll stay here with Houston, and the rest of you can go on ahead. We'll meet up with you when we're finished here."

Jake looked at me. "Are you up for trying to connect while we're waiting for Dani?"

A headache started to develop, and I wanted to say no, but I knew how important this was. I assured Jake I'd try and then looked around for a quiet and comfortable place to get settled. Houston offered to act as my anchor, which I greatly appreciated. I was sure that any of the others would help if asked, but with the exception of Jake, who'd been with me since day one, Houston had more experience than the others did.

"If you don't feel up to it, you can say no," Houston reminded me once we were well away from the others.

"I know, but this is important. I know that even if my head feels like it's going to explode, it won't, and while the headache won't be fun at the time, I'll recover."

I found a comfortable place to sit and then I studied my copy of the photo of the teens Jake had given to everyone. I committed the image of Logan to my mind and then closed my eyes. I decided on Logan since, as Jake had pointed out, he had a lot of responsibility in all of this and was more likely than the other males to be feeling the pressure of trying to keep his cousin and girlfriend safe, but while I'd had a glimmer of something the last time I'd tried, I came up with nothing this time. After fifteen minutes, I tried again with Brit. Based on what I knew about her, she seemed like she would be brave and adventurous, so if I could find my way to the door in her mind, maybe she'd be brave enough to open the door and let me in.

"I think I may be in," I said. "I can feel a presence, but I can't see anything." I focused in on her harder. "Brit?" I asked, not knowing with any certainty that hers was the mind I'd connected with. "If you're there and can hear me, my name is Harmony. I'm on the mountain with the search and rescue team. We're at the campsite, the first campsite at Glacier Lake. If you hear me in your head, all you need to do to respond is to think about what you want to say."

An image of Braydon flashed through my mind. I had to assume the image had actually been generated in Brit's mind, but I supposed that the image could have piggybacked on my intent and that any of the teens could have been thinking about Braydon at that moment in time.

My eyes flew open.

"What is it?" Houston asked.

"I think those teens might be in a lot more trouble than we ever imagined."

"Why? What did you see?"

"The image that flashed through my mind was of Brayden. At least, I think it was Braydon based on hair color and body build. I couldn't see his face, but Braydon is blond, and the others have darker hair."

"What was he doing?" Houston asked.

"He was lying on the ground, face down. There was blood everywhere. Since he was lying on his stomach, I wasn't sure if he'd been shot, stabbed, or hit in the head with a heavy object, but there was a lot of blood, and he wasn't moving."

"Did the person you connected with say anything?" Houston wondered.

"No. There was just a flash of the image of the boy with blond hair lying face down on the ground. I had an image of blood. It wasn't a large pool of blood like you might find if someone bled out, but there was definitely blood in the picture. I tried to focus in closer, but the connection was broken as quickly as it appeared. I don't know with any degree of certainty who I was connected with. I was trying for Brit, but you know how this works. My intention to connect isn't always enough. It's entirely possible that I connected with one of the others."

Houston stood up. "I'm not sure it matters who shared the image. If Braydon is injured or worse, that adds additional urgency to this situation. How long do you think it will take for Dani to get here with our supplies?"

I looked up into the sky. "I don't see Dani yet, but I know she knew to hurry. I suspect she'll be here soon. She can't land on this side of the lake, so we'll need to hike around. We should get going. It makes sense to be at the landing site when she arrives."

"Does this happen often?" he asked. "Is it common for the team to start out on a search and rescue thinking they're taking on a day hike and then find something that causes them to stay longer?"

"Does it happen often?" I asked as we walked back toward the campsite. "No. Has it happened occasionally? Yes. Not so much with winter rescues. In the winter, we limit our exposure whether we find our victim or not. In fact, we usually work in shifts so that the rescue can continue even if each team member is limited in the amount of time they can work before being required to take a break. But there have been summer rescues that have turned into multi-day events. Not a lot, but a few."

"I don't think you've mentioned something like this occurring since I've been living in Alaska."

"It's been a while since the entire team was pulled into something so complex."

Once Houston and I arrived at the campsite, we all walked around the lake to greet Dani. I wasn't sure what the image I had received meant or even if it was factual rather than simply a figment of someone's imagination, but it did seem that the urgency we all felt had increased exponentially once we realized that at least one of the teens was either seriously hurt or dead.

Once we received our supplies, it was decided that Jake, Wyatt, and I would continue moving forward with the three dogs while Landon helped Houston gather samples and evidence. After Houston and Landon had done what they could to process the campsite, Dani would take the samples and evidence to town for processing, and Landon and Houston would rejoin the larger group.

"Do you have an idea of the direction you'll take?" Landon asked as we divided the supplies that would need to be carried among the team members.

Jake answered. "As far as we know, the teens planned to head to Aloha Lake once they left Glacier Lake, but now that a ninth person is involved, it's hard to say where the group is headed. At this point, all we can do is follow the footprints. We'll stay in touch via our radios and satellite phones."

"On a positive note, the items left behind at Glacier Lake will provide a fresh scent for the dogs to follow," Wyatt said.

Wyatt was right. The dogs did seem a lot more active than they'd been during the first leg of our journey.

After we left Glacier Lake, Jake, Wyatt, and I spread out a little bit, putting a football field between us. The landscape was hilly and rocky, making traveling in a straight line impossible, but we'd decided to do the best we could while keeping a line of sight between Jake and ourselves, who headed up the middle.

The distance between Glacier Lake and Aloha Lake was only about five miles, but it was five miles that traveled first straight up the side of a mountain and then straight down into a crater that had been formed long before there were humans in the area to worry about maintaining trails in the rocky terrain.

"It seems counterintuitive to me that the person who wrecked the campsite at Glacier Lake would take the teens to the very lake that had been part of their initial itinerary," Wyatt said as we walked side by side once the trail he'd been walking had come to an end at a steep drop off.

"It does seem that if the person who wrecked the campsite also kidnapped the teens, then he or she would head off in a different direction from the one the group had determined ahead of time," I agreed. "The main question in my mind, however, isn't so much which direction did the person behind the missing teens head in, as it is why this individual kidnapped at least seven of the teens."

"So, do you think Braydon died before the group ever left Glacier Lake?"

"I think he may have. One of the tents was left behind, as was one of the backpacks. It would make sense that one set of supplies and equipment would be left behind if it was no longer needed."

"So why didn't we find a body?" Wyatt asked as we neared the location where we would join Jake.

"I don't know," I admitted. "Maybe Braydon didn't die at the campsite. Maybe he isn't even dead, and the image I saw in my vision was pure fiction. I certainly don't have all the answers, but my intuition is telling me that Braydon likely left the others before they continued on from Glacier Lake."

We joined Jake as we headed up the steep side of the mountain. I wasn't sure why we were even taking this route. The dogs seemed to have lost the scent, and we'd already discussed the fact that it seemed unlikely that the teens would continue with their original itinerary. I supposed we simply needed a direction to head in, and Aloha Lake made as much sense as anywhere.

"This is a good place to stop," Jake said as we neared the top of the mountain. "Once we start down, we won't be able to communicate with Houston and Landon via the radio."

"They should be on their way by now," I said.

"We have several hours of daylight left, so I'm going to suggest we wait for them to catch up, and then we can all descend into the crater together," Jake said. He looked at me. "In the meantime, maybe you can take a break and try to connect with one of the teens again. If we're heading in the wrong direction, it would be nice to know that before we make the strenuous climb down and then have to climb back out of the crater."

I nodded. "Okay. I'm going to grab some water and a granola bar, and then I'll try. I only need to connect with one of the teens in order to attempt to figure out a direction. Even if the teen doesn't know where they currently are, they should be able to tell me whether or not they descended into the crater."

"That's what I'm hoping."

"Houston to Jake," Houston said over the radio just as I was about to slide my backpack off in anticipation of taking a break.

"Go for Jake," Jake responded.

"We're at the foot of the mountain about to start up, and we decided to take a break. We were looking for a good place to rest when we found a blue baseball cap. I checked the photo you provided and discovered that Pete was wearing a blue cap."

"That sounds right," Jake said. "Maybe he lost it while he was hiking."

"There's blood on the hat, Jake. A lot of it."

My heart sank.

Houston continued. "Landon noticed footprints in the mud heading off to the west. You wouldn't have noticed them if you'd stuck to the trail heading up the mountain. We only noticed them because we left the trail to find a flat rock in a shady spot to catch a breather. Landon and I discussed it, and we think we should follow the footprints, although there appears to be only a single set. It looks like the rest of the group is headed up the mountain. If someone split off from the group, it appears this is where they may have done so. Landon and I are thinking of following the footprints, but it would help to have Kojak."

Jake looked at Wyatt and me.

"I can take Kojak down the mountain," Wyatt said. "Maybe you and Harm should set up camp here. Harmony can work on trying to connect with one of the teens while Houston, Landon, and I check out the footprints they discovered."

Jake looked at his watch. "You have about four hours of daylight."

"The trip down the mountain will be fast. We'll look around and then head back. I'd say that you and Harmony could head down into the crater, but if you do that, we won't be able to communicate."

"There was a flat spot at the bottom of the mountain just before we began to climb," I said. "It makes the most sense to me that the three of us head back to set up camp there. One of you can head out with Kojak to help follow the footprints, and I'll stay behind with whoever wants to stay with me and try to connect."

Jake hesitated.

"The climb up was steep and took a while, but the climb back down should be accomplished in an hour max," I pointed out.

"Okay," Jake finally said. "That sounds like a good idea. If the teens are camping at Aloha Lake, the plan will delay getting to them by a day, but if there's a hurt teen out there who took off on his own, I suppose at this point, finding him might be the most important thing."

Jake radioed Landon with the plan, and the three of us and the three dogs started back down the trail we'd just finished climbing.

Chapter 3

By the time Jake, Wyatt, the dogs, and I made our way back down the mountain, Houston and Landon had followed the footprints and found Pete. He'd been stabbed and left for dead. The coroner would need to determine the cause of death in order to be sure, but based on the amount of blood on the ground and the fact that the men had followed a blood trail for a while before discovering the body, we suspected that Pete was stabbed and ran until he eventually fell to the ground and had simply bled out.

"What in the heck is going on up here?" I asked as I wiped a tear from my cheek. I didn't know Pete and had never even met him, but a death during a rescue, any death, always seemed to claw at my emotions.

"You said you saw a flash of a person laying on the ground in a pool of blood in your vision," Houston said. "Are you sure it wasn't this body?"

I shook my head. "The boy in my vision had blond hair and a blue shirt. I wasn't able to see the victim's face, so I can't even be sure the individual in the vision was one of the teens we're looking for but based on the photo Jake gave me, if it was one of the teens, I'm pretty sure it was Braydon."

"So whoever joined the teens back at the last campsite is killing these teens for some reason," Houston said.

"We need help," Jake said. "I'm going to reach out to other search and rescue groups in Northern Alaska. Houston, you should see if you can get additional law enforcement up here."

"Way ahead of you," Houston said. "I put in a call to the Fairbanks PD, and they're sending a team. Dani said she can deliver them wherever we need them to be as long as there's a place for her to land."

Jake looked at me. "So, how about it?"

I knew what he was asking, and I nodded. Once again, I looked for a quiet spot and tried to connect with anyone who might be receptive to my presence. Our ability to contact one another via radio was limited due to the tall mountains in the area, but similar obstacles didn't seem to limit my psychic ability. To date, there had been a limitation in terms of overall proximity, but even that distance seemed to grow as my gift, as a whole, expanded.

I sat down in a quiet space and closed my eyes. I felt as if the individual I'd connected with briefly during my prior attempt might have been Brit, although I didn't know this with any degree of certainty. The joining had been an arm's length connection where I briefly saw a flash of something the person I'd linked with had seen, but I didn't sense that this individual necessarily knew I was there rooting around in his or her head.

It took a good fifteen minutes before I got anything, but I was eventually able to sense darkness. I wasn't sure if I was sensing a void or if the person I connected with was in a shadowy place. I didn't think I could learn much from this connection, but then I heard someone whisper.

"How long do we need to stay here?" a female voice said so quietly it was barely audible.

"We need to stay until we're sure he's gone," another female answered.

"Shhh," someone else said. "He'll hear."

With that, the connection was gone.

I opened my eyes and looked around for Houston or Jake. I could hear voices in the distance. I knew that Jake had called Dani to bring the chopper. There was a place to land about half a mile from where we'd set up camp, so the men were going to carry Pete's body to the field and wait for Dani, who would pick the teen up and then deliver him to the coroner.

Getting up from my resting place, I went in search of Houston. He was talking to Wyatt as they wrapped the body in one of the sleeping bags. I wasn't sure how smart it was to give up one of our sleeping bags, but I understood the need to cover him.

"The officers from Fairbanks PD will be here at some point after sunrise," Houston informed us. It was about an hour until sunset early at this time of the year, we'd have a short time to rest before we needed to head out again. "They're going to catch a ride with Dani after she has a chance to deliver Pete's body to the coroner, fuel the chopper, and rest up a bit."

"Dani should be here in about five minutes to collect Pete's body," Jake informed the group. "She's bringing a replacement sleeping bag for the one we used to cover the victim, along with a few additional supplies." He looked at Landon, Wyatt, and me. "The three of you should take the dogs and head back to the campsite to get the tents set up and a fire going. Houston and I will wait with the body until we can make the handoff to Dani."

I supposed I'd need to wait to tell Houston what I'd seen until after Dani left with Pete's body, and we all settled in around the fire, which everyone knew was necessary both for warmth and as a wild animal deterrent.

The next hour flew by quickly. Dani arrived, and Pete's body was loaded into the chopper. I'd decided to sit down, close my eyes, and try to quell the explosion that was about to occur in my head.

"Are you okay?" Landon asked after joining me.

I looked up. "I'm okay. A little headache, but I'll be fine. I figured I'd try to get some rest while we wait for the officers Fairbanks PD is sending to help Houston. Did Dani say when she thought she might be back?"

"She didn't say, but I know she needs to fuel up and grab a few hours rest after she delivers the body, so I don't expect it to be too early."

"We need to find some money in the budget for the fuel she's using with all the flying back and forth."

"Jake will make sure she's compensated," Landon assured me. "Wyatt is making freeze-dried stew if you're hungry."

"Actually, I'm starving, and the stew is one of the better freeze-dried options."

"Dani had a loaf of bread in the chopper that she left with us as well, so we even have something for dipping."

Landon reached his hand out and pulled me to my feet. I could see that the tents were set up, and the fire was blazing cheerily. An overnight camping trip with some of my favorite people was something I'd usually enjoy very much, but all I could think about at this moment was the group I'd briefly looked in on who were huddled in the dark, scared to so much as move lest the person who killed Pete choose one of them to be his next victim.

I accepted the bowl of stew and bread Landon handed me and then sat down on a log. Yukon had been curled up with Sitka and Kojak, but when I sat down, he wandered over to sit at my feet. If I were honest with myself, the real reason he left his buddies to come and sit with me likely had to do with the bowl of stew in my hands, but I liked to think he sensed that I needed a cuddly buddy by my side and wanted to be there for me in my time of need.

"Any luck?" Jake asked after I'd finished eating.

"Actually, yes. I was able to connect with someone briefly. I'm not sure who I connected with, and the connection didn't last long, but I heard voices. Female voices."

"We're you able to identify whose voices you heard?" Houston asked.

"No. It was dark, so I wasn't able to see anyone. I don't know if the girls were in a dark space or if I was picking up audio but not video for some reason. But I heard one girl commenting about wondering how long they needed to wait, and another girl said until they were sure he was gone. Then a third female voice shushed them because she feared someone would hear them. If I had to guess, at least two of the missing female teens we're looking for are holed up somewhere. Somewhere dark. Maybe a cave."

"I feel like we're wasting time just sitting here," Houston said with a tone of impatience that was actually very un-Houston-like. "I know I need to wait for the officers from Fairbanks, but maybe we should have figured out a way to get them here sooner or to meet them at a location further along the trail."

"It's never a good idea to set out in the dark," Jake cautioned. "I know it can be hard to wait, especially when we know lives are in danger, but the safety of the search and rescue team has to come first. I'm going to suggest that we all get some sleep and wait for both the sun to rise and the recruits you have coming. Once they arrive, we'll come up with a plan to find those teens."

Houston blew out a breath of frustration. "Yeah. You're right, of course."

"It seems obvious that the teens deviated from their original plan," Wyatt said. "Should we even waste our time going all the way to Aloha Lake? With the rough terrain and the gear we're carrying, it's going to be a half-day round trip."

"Let's talk about it in the morning," Jake suggested. He seemed calm and operating from a place of logic and not emotion. "Maybe Harmony can make a better connection once she has a chance to rest up a bit. If the teens didn't go to Aloha Lake, which I imagine we are all assuming at this point, then I agree that making the trip would be a waste of time. I hate to skip it on a whim, but it is a pretty specific trail with steep terrain. Anyone who hiked it would remember doing so, so if Harmony can make a two-way connection before we leave here, maybe she can simply ask whoever she connects with if they went that way."

Everyone agreed to Jake's plan, but the additional stress it put on me to be "the one" to figure out what to do next had my head pounding even worse than it had been. Houston offered to share a tent with me, Wyatt and Landon planned to share, and Jake planned to share his space with the dogs. Initially, I'd planned to keep Yukon with me, but snuggling up with

Houston didn't sound half bad, so when the sleeping arrangements were announced, I happily went along with the plan.

Chapter 4

"Harm, are you awake?" Houston asked me a few hours later. The sun had risen, and the sky was bright. "The chopper is here, so I'm going to meet it."

"Okay," I said, sitting up and looking around. I hadn't thought I'd be able to sleep, but I must have since I couldn't remember a thing after I'd turned on my side and Houston had looped his arm over my waist from behind. We were each in our own sleeping bag, so it was a move made to ensure optimal heat utilization rather than any sort of intimacy, but when the weight of his arm pressed into my body, all I could feel was contentment.

"I heard Jake say something about breakfast, and I can smell coffee, so I'm going to suggest that you get up and eat before I get back with the recruits."

"I will," I said. "And thank you."

He raised a brow. "For what?"

"For creating a safe space so I could sleep. I actually feel much better. I'm going to grab some coffee and something to eat, check on the dogs, and try to connect again."

"I'm going to feed Kojak and then take him with me to meet the others. The hike to the clearing to greet the officers from Fairbanks weaves through some pretty thick brush. I think I'll feel better with him along to act as an alarm should there be grizzly bears or wolves in the area."

"That's not a bad idea, but have your gun loaded and ready as well."

"Always."

Houston unzipped the tent and slipped out. Yukon came trotting in while I was pulling on my outerwear and boots. "Did you have fun sleeping with Jake and your buddies?"

He wagged his tail and licked my face.

"I would have let you in here, but these are really small tents."

Yukon let out a friendly yip.

I crawled out of the tent into the early morning sunshine. The fire was going, and I could see the coffee pot on the camp stove, so I made my way in that direction.

"Did you have a good night's sleep?" Wyatt asked with a smirk on his face. I knew he wanted to tease me about sharing a tent with Houston, but I wasn't in the mood and ignored the invitation to participate in whatever banter he had planned.

"It was only a few hours, so I'm not sure I'd call it a good night's sleep, but I did sleep, and I do feel better," I informed him. "I'm going to have some coffee, and then I'm going to try to connect again. If we can get a clear picture of where the survivors are holed up, that will cut down the length of this search considerably."

Wyatt was the sort who loved to tease, but he must have sensed that I wasn't in the mood since he left me alone while I downed my first cup of coffee. Once I'd nibbled on an apple and a muffin and finished my second cup of coffee, I found a quiet place to sit and tried to connect with anyone who would open their mind to me.

"Brit?" I asked when I finally felt a presence after trying to connect for at least twenty minutes.

"Who are you?" she whispered.

"My name is Harmony, and I'm speaking to you with my mind. There's no need for you to speak. If you want to communicate with me, just think of the words you want to say."

"How are you doing this?"

"I'll explain later," I said in my mind. "Right now, I need to find you and the others. Do you know where you are?"

"No."

"Are you okay?"

"Not even slightly."

Okay, I figured as much. "I'm not sure how long we'll have until the link is broken, so what can you tell me that might help us find you?"

There was a long pause, but she eventually answered. "We were camping at Glacier Lake. This man came into the campsite and asked where Hope was. We told him that we didn't know anyone named Hope and that he likely had the wrong group, but he got super agitated. Braydon tried to stop him when he began tearing apart the campsite looking for Hope, but the man pulled a knife out and cut him. Braydon took off running. I'm not sure if he's dead or alive. We never saw him again. After Braydon took off, Pete tried to follow him, but the man pulled a gun out. He told us he'd start shooting if we didn't all freeze and stay where we were. We were scared, so we did as he demanded."

"And then?" I asked, realizing we needed to send someone back to find Braydon or Braydon's body, as the case may be.

"And then he tied us all to each other. He had a long rope and tied our wrists to the rope with a bit of spacing between us so we could walk. Once we were all tied to the rope, he tied the other end around his waist. He told us that we needed to find Hope. He said that no one was leaving until he had her. After that, he just made us walk aimlessly for days. There didn't seem to be any sort of plan in play. We just walked from one place to another while he looked for

Hope. After a few days, we were so exhausted and weak from all the walking and lack of food that we decided to risk an escape. We came up with a plan that included Pete finding something to hit the guy over the head with. We were going to attack him while he slept and then cut the rope and run. The problem was that the man woke up and stabbed Pete before Pete could hit him."

I could feel the pain this young girl was going through and found the connection almost too much to maintain, but still, I hung on.

"Where are you now?"

"In a cave. After Pete was hurt, the man looking for Hope made us walk in a different direction. I'm pretty sure we ended up on the back side of Aloha Lake. Not down in the crater but on the other side of the mountain. We were all so weak and scared by this point. The rope around Logan's wrists was loose, and he managed to work his hands free. When we stopped to rest, Logan helped Carter get his hands free. Logan used a knife he had in his pocket to cut the rope so that Carrie, Alice, Talia, and I could get free, and then told us to run while he and Carter attacked the man who held us captive."

"And where did you run to?"

"I don't know. A cave. We just ran when Logan told us to. We didn't pay a lot of attention to direction. Eventually, Talia noticed a cave. We made our way inside and have been hiding for at least a couple days."

"And Logan and Carter?"

She began to cry. "I don't know. We could hear yelling and screaming as we ran away, but none of us looked back. Logan told us to run, so we did."

"Do you have a reason to believe that the man who took you is still in the area?" I asked.

"A few hours after we hid in the cave, we heard him outside. He was calling for Hope. He seems to have moved on, but we've heard a lot of strange sounds that might be animals. We talked about looking outside, but before we do, we wanted to be sure the noises we heard weren't being made by the crazy man who seemed to want to kill us for some reason."

I was getting weak and could feel the connection fading. I told Brit I had to go but that I'd be back. I assured her that people were looking for them and that we'd find them as soon as we could. I instructed her to wait and listen for me to come back again. I hoped to have a list of instructions when I returned. What we needed was a plan that would allow us to find the girls while not leading the madman who had held them hostage right back to them.

As the connection faded, I willed her to be brave. As my vision went blank, I prayed that she'd be safe. I couldn't imagine sitting in a dark, damp cave waiting for someone who may have just killed your friends to find you. I wanted to offer her something solid to hang onto, but all I could offer was my promise to do the best that I could.

Chapter 5

When Houston returned with the officers from Fairbanks, we all gathered together to discuss the situation. I shared what Brit had told me, which didn't go over all that well with the visiting officers who thought I was crazy. After a bit of discussion, it was decided that the new recruits would hike back toward Glacier Lake and try to find Braydon's body. While I hoped they'd find Braydon alive, the reality was that it had been days since he'd taken off alone and without supplies, and even if he hadn't been injured, it was unlikely that he would survive long being out in the elements. Given the fact that he'd been bleeding, it seemed highly likely the mission would be a recovery.

The officers from Fairbanks, whose names I didn't catch, had radios and satellite phones and were instructed to contact Dani once they found Braydon, whether he was dead or alive. Dani would then arrange to bring the chopper and transport the patient or the body back to Fairbanks. In the meantime, Dani was going to do flyovers, hoping to get close enough to the cave where the girls were hiding that they could hear her.

So far, we knew that Pete was dead, and we suspected that Braydon was likewise gone. Brit didn't know what had happened to Logan and Carter, but I had to admit, if only to myself, that I was going to be amazed if either boy survived. I supposed it was possible that the boys had managed to get free and had taken off running the same way the girls had, but given the fact that they stayed behind to fight off their kidnapper, it seemed somewhat unlikely.

"So how, other than asking Dani to fly over thousands of square miles of trees, mountains, and ravines, are we going to find these teens?" Landon asked.

Jake looked at me. "What do you think? Perhaps if you can persuade Brit to leave the cave, even if just for a few minutes, she can look around and provide us with a landmark or something we can use as a starting point."

"I'll try," I said. "But Brit is weak, and my head is pounding. I'll do what I can, but I can't promise anything."

"All I'm asking you to do is to try," Jake said.

I nodded, took a deep breath, and found a place to sit. Even though Brit was a healthy young athlete, I could sense how weak she was. So, if she was beginning to fade, I could only imagine the shape we'd find the other teens in.

"Brit," I said in my mind. I envisioned the smiling face in the photo and reached out to her with my whole heart and mind. "Are you there? Can you hear me? It's Harmony again. We're going to come for you, but first, we need to find you."

My first, second, and third attempts were met with total silence. I wanted to give up, especially since I suspected that Brit may have either died or slipped into an unconscious state, but she was strong, and I was determined, so I kept at it.

"Come on, Brit. Help me out here. I need you to let me in."

I took a deep breath, focused my energy, and offered up the last of my strength.

"Harmony?"

"It's me," I said, a wave of relief washing over me. "How are you?" I could tell that she was getting weaker by the minute, and I knew we needed to find those girls and find them fast.

"I'm okay."

"How are the others doing?" I asked once I'd assured myself that Brit could read me and had willingly let me in.

"We're all getting weak, but we're still alive. Carrie mostly sleeps. She's worried about Carter, and I think that she's all but given up. Talia and I are okay. Alice has been coughing. I think she might be sick."

"I know this is hard, but we will find you. The thing is that since your group aimlessly wandered after the man kidnapped and led you away from Glacier Lake, it's hard for us to pick up your trail. I need you to help me figure out where you are."

"As I already told you, I don't know where we are."

"I realize that, but if we had some landmarks as points of reference, I think we'll be able to figure out where you are. I don't blame you for being frightened, but I need you to go outside and look around. In the past, I've been able to see what those I'm connected with can see. I'm not a hundred percent sure it will work since all I can see is darkness right now, but since you're in a dark cave, the fact that I can't see anything doesn't mean that I won't be able to once you are out in the sunlight."

"What if the man who kidnapped us is still here?"

I hesitated. I could sense the fear in the girl's voice, and the last thing I wanted to do was to send her into the arms of a killer, but we really did need something to go on if we had any chance of finding them. "You said before that you'd been hiding in the cave for a couple days."

"Yes. I don't know for certain, but that would be my guess." She paused and then continued. "The passage of time in the dark is difficult to determine. The man took our cell phones and smartwatches when he tied us up, so we don't know how much time has passed. It feels like we've been here forever, but I suspect it's actually been two days."

"You left for your trip ten days ago. Do you remember how many days passed before you ran into the cave?"

She paused. "It took us two days to hike up to Glacier Lake because Pete had a blister and had to keep stopping to rest. Once we got there, we set up camp. The man showed up on our third day at the lake, so that was two nights at the lake and one on the trail before he arrived. He tied us up, and we began walking. I guess we walked aimlessly for another three or four days before the guys decided to make their move, which must mean we've been here in this cave for two days. Maybe three. As I said, I'm not sure exactly."

"Chances are that if you've been in the cave for two or three days and he hasn't found you, then the man has moved on. I still need you to move slowly and be extra cautious, but our best chance of getting to you today is for you to help me figure out where you are."

"Okay. I'll do as you say."

I could sense that she stood up. She told the others that she was going to peek outside but would be back. There was only one reply, which, in my mind, meant that the other two were likely asleep, unconscious, or dead.

When Brit first emerged from the cave, and her eyes met sunlight, I wanted to scream with the pain. She closed her eyes and retreated back into the cave a bit until the pain from the sunlight was subdued, and then she continued forward slowly, allowing time for her eyes to adjust to the light. When she was finally free of the cave, I instructed her to turn slowly in a circle. As I'd hoped, I was able to see what she could see, which meant that once I got my bearings, I should be able to figure out where the girls were hiding.

"Okay, stop turning and stand still, so I can get my bearings."

She did as I instructed.

"Turn your head to the right."

She did as I asked.

"It looks like the Collins Glacier is to your right. Based on the angle of the sun, I'm going to assume that your right is east. If the glacier is to your east, then the mountain peak in front of you should be Hallelujah Ridge. Turn slightly and look to your left. What do you see?"

"Trees."

"Yeah, I can't see much either. Is there a river beyond the trees?" I asked.

"I can hear one, but I can't see one." She looked around. "I feel sort of vulnerable out here."

"I know. We're almost done. What's behind you?"

"Rocks. The cave where we are hiding is hidden in the rocks."

"Okay, that's very good. I feel like I have a general idea of where you're hiding. Do you see anything that will narrow things down a bit more?"

"There's a large dead tree with a fork about a hundred yards east of the opening to the cave. If you get this far, you won't miss it."

"Do you know how far you ran after you escaped your captor?"

"No. We just ran. I remember hiking around to the back side of the crater where Aloha Lake is located before this whole thing went down. I remember walking into the sun that morning, so we must have been heading east. That should give you a general idea of where we were when Logan and Carter decided to confront the man."

"Okay. I'm going to grab a map and try to figure out a search grid. Our helicopter pilot will be making sweeps in the area, so if you hear a chopper, come outside and wave it down."

"What if it's not your pilot?"

"It will be. Based on what you told me, the man who took you is on foot, so it's unlikely he has a chopper."

"That's true. I'll listen for it. And Harmony…"

"Yeah?"

"Hurry. I've been having a hard time waking Carrie up, and when I tried to wake Alice right before I came out here, I realized that she's burning up."

"We're on our way. Just hang on a little while longer."

By the time I returned to the group, the officers from Fairbanks had left to look for Braydon, and the others had broken down the camp. Jake had a map laid out on the ground, and everyone in the group was standing around it. I pointed to the landmarks I'd seen through Brit's eyes. I described the location where she remembered the showdown between the kidnapper and the boys taking place, and we tried to use this information to determine where the girls might have ended up. The area we were able to narrow things down to was huge, but between the dogs, who we hoped would pick up a scent, and Dani's birdseye view, we hoped we'd have enough to bring the four girls home safely.

The hike to the general area where we believed Brit and the others were holed up wasn't going to be easy. There was a mountain ridge to both ascend and descend, a river to cross, and an unstable glacier to navigate. We discussed having Dani drop someone closer to our goal, but given the trees and terrain, she wouldn't be able to land, and parachuting in would be dangerous. At this point, staying together and sticking to the plan seemed the safest choice currently available to us.

"I wonder if we should have someone with access to a computer try to figure out who the man who took these teens is," I said. "We don't know a lot about him, but we know he was looking for someone named Hope. Perhaps we can radio Sarge and have him search the records for a missing person named Hope."

"That might not be a bad idea," Houston said. "Knowing what motivates this guy might be good information to have should we run into him at some point. I'll radio my office and see if anyone is available who can look for missing person reports, but if Sarge has time, we should get him on it as well."

"You won't have any reception as long as we're down in this ravine, but we're going to start climbing that mountain once we cross the river, so you should be able to get through from there," I said.

"And how exactly are we going to cross the river?" Houston asked.

"There's a swinging bridge that someone built for backpackers. As long as it wasn't washed out over the winter, we should be able to get across that way. If not, then we'll need to hike farther north where the river narrows at the falls."

"Falls?" Houston asked.

"Don't worry. Most who attempt the crossing make it okay."

I knew Houston was a brave man who risked his life on a regular basis, but for some reason, the idea of crossing the currently raging river seemed to have him spooked. Maybe he'd had a bad experience with a river crossing. A single negative experience could leave a permanent scar that sometimes leads to fears and phobias beyond the norm. I personally feared garden snails to the point that I'd go running if I came across one. I wasn't sure where my repulsion came from, but I suspect there was a story that would explain my tendency to freak out if one crossed my path.

When we reached the river, we found the bridge intact. It was a dicey crossing for sure, but it was the best way to proceed, so it was the option we needed to take.

"Are you sure that will hold?" Houston asked. "The river is raging less than six inches beneath the rotted timber that was used to build the darn thing in the first place."

"It'll hold," I assured the man. "I'm going to take Yukon across, and then Jake will follow with Sitka. I'll come back for you while Wyatt takes Kojak."

"I'm sure I can make it on my own," Houston said in a voice that made it apparent that I'd offended his manhood.

I shrugged. "Okay. But be sure you have a good grip on Kojak. He's a new S&R dog who hasn't been in this situation before. We don't want him to panic."

"I've got this," Houston assured me. "You just worry about getting Yukon across safely."

Once Jake and I got our dogs and ourselves across, Wyatt suggested that Houston and Kojak go next. Luckily, the crossing went smoothly, so once Landon and Wyatt had traversed the river, we headed up the mountain, where we hoped to find an area that was unobstructed that would not only allow us to use the radio to check in with Dani and the officers from Fairbanks but contact Sarge and Houston's office as well.

"It looks like there's another hiker in the area," Jake announced once we'd settled in for a break in a large meadow at the top of the mountain.

I looked in the direction that Jake was pointing. The smoke from a fire was curling into the blue sky, indicating that we, in fact, were not alone. We were in a pretty isolated location, but it wasn't unreasonable that others were out for a wilderness adventure. The fire was too far from the area where we'd determined the girls in hiding were waiting for us to be one of them, but it did enter my mind that it could be the man who killed at least one of the teens and likely four rather than hikers.

"Should we check it out?" I asked Houston.

"No," he answered. "Our priority needs to be to find the missing teens before it's too late. Once we've rescued those we can and have returned the bodies of those we couldn't rescue to their families, I'll need to develop a plan to track this man down."

"Maybe you should close the area to hiking and camping until we catch up with him," Landon suggested. "It's occurred to me that this guy might kidnap others he runs across now that he's either lost or killed the hostages he had."

"I can do that. I suspect that there will be those who ignore the closure, but I can spread the word that a killer is on the loose in the area, and folks should stay clear of this particular wilderness area until he's captured."

"Chances are that making an announcement like that will only draw people to the area," Wyatt said.

Wyatt was right. You'd think that, as human beings, we'd have an innate sense of self-preservation that would prevent us from intentionally putting ourselves in danger. But I'd been doing this job long enough to know that an increase in personal risks, such as a rogue grizzly bear or an overactive pack of wolves, only seemed to increase the number of visitors to the area looking for an adventure to tell their grandkids about in the future. I'd spoken to men and women who'd fallen victim to the very danger we'd warned them could be a problem, and they'd all responded by saying that they were careful and hadn't thought anything bad could happen to them. One could never be careful enough when it came to a killer animal, whether that animal was a bear or a man. If you got in his way, he would kill you no matter how invincible you might feel.

Chapter 6

After making our calls, we hiked down the back side of the mountain. The officers from Fairbanks hadn't found Braydon's body yet, but they were still looking. Sarge agreed to do what he could to track down someone in the area who might be looking for an individual named Hope, one of the officers in Houston's office was going to look into missing person reports, and Dani reported that she'd been doing a grid all morning with zero success. Dani was heading back to the airport but would return to her flyovers once she had a chance to grab a bite to eat and fuel the bird.

Brit had said that the showdown between the man who kidnapped them and the young men who tried to save them had taken place on the back side of the crater near Aloha Lake. There was only one trail down the back side of the tall peak, so we hoped that we'd find something left behind that would provide a scent for the dogs to follow once we made it to the bottom. The girls had run, leaving the boys behind, so in addition to blood, clothing, or something else that would serve as a scent, we fully expected to find the bodies of both Carter Harding and Logan Burge.

"Let's split up and take a few minutes to look around," Jake said once we reached the clearing where a struggle appeared to have taken place. "I don't want to waste a lot of time here, but if there was a struggle, chances are that there's something to find."

After about ten minutes, Sitka alerted. Jake followed her to a heavily wooded area where the body of one of the boys was lying next to a fallen log. Based on the photo, it appeared the teen who died was seventeen-year-old Carter Harding. Carter had a gash on his forehead and scratches on his arms and legs. It didn't look like he'd been shot or stabbed, and based on his injuries, it appeared that he'd put up quite a fight.

Even though we all assumed he was dead, Jake knelt down to check for a pulse. My heart ached for Carter and the survivors who'd have to live with his death. I remembered that Carrie and Carter had been dating and suspected she would be deeply affected by his death.

"I have a pulse," Jake said. "It's weak, but it's there. We need to call Dani. This boy needs to get to a hospital now."

I looked around. "There are peaks all around us. I doubt we'll be able to get a call out from our current location. We're basically in a hole. We need to get high enough above the peaks to find an unobstructed airway between Dani and us."

"I'll climb back up the crater until I can get a signal," Wyatt offered. "If Dani is in the air, I may not have to go all the way to the top."

"Okay, but hurry," Jake said before turning to the rest of us. "Dani isn't going to be able to land down here with all the trees. We need to gather supplies and build a stretcher of some sort to carry Carter to a location where Dani can land." Jake looked at me. "Harm, you and Houston look for a place that's accessible and will accommodate the bird. The closer to our location, the better, but it has to be well away from the trees. Keep an eye out for drafts created by the steep cliff faces. Landon and I will find materials to build a stretcher. Hopefully, this boy can hang on long enough for us to get him out of here and into the hands of someone who can help him."

Houston and I found a small meadow about half a mile from where we'd found Carter. The meadow was far enough away from the walls of the surrounding cliffs not to be affected by random drafts created by the sheer drop offs. By the time we hiked back to fill Jake in on what we'd found, Jake and Landon had a stretcher ready. They'd already rolled Carter onto the makeshift backboard and were monitoring his respiration and heart rate. Houston went to find Wyatt to give him the location of the meadow while Jake and Landon moved Carter to the meadow to wait for Dani to arrive, and I followed with the dogs. Houston and Wyatt showed up about five minutes after we arrived at the meadow with Carter.

"Do you think there is any chance this boy will make it to the hospital alive?" Wyatt asked, breathing hard after his run up and then back down the mountain.

Jake felt for a pulse once again. "Probably not, but we have to try. He's made it this long, so maybe he can hang on a little longer."

"Any idea when Dani will be here?" I asked.

"Soon," Wyatt answered. "Dani's been in the air doing flyovers and was close. She said she'd be here within twenty minutes, and that was eighteen minutes ago."

I looked up and watched as the helicopter flew into view. Once Dani arrived, the rescue went smoothly. We felt that someone should go with Dani and Carter in the chopper should it be necessary to administer CPR on the way, so Landon volunteered to go. The plan was for Dani and Landon to take the teen to the hospital, and then Dani would bring Landon back to a location we'd identified as a good place to regroup. The clearing where Dani met us and took possession of Carter was quite a few miles from where we suspected the girls were holed up. Our plan was to look for a place where Dani could land once she returned from the hospital, and then we'd send one or two of us up with her while the others continued on foot with the dogs.

"I still can't believe that boy was alive," Wyatt said as we continued toward the location where we'd planned to meet Dani and Landon later that day.

"He had a pulse, but I'm not sure he'll make it," Jake said. "He lost a lot of blood, and it's likely been a couple days since he's had water."

"He made it this far, so we'll just hope for the best," I reminded Jake of the exact thing he'd just told us about the sheer will of this very strong boy.

"It's tough when a rescue turns into a recovery," Wyatt commented. "At this point, I know it's in our best interest, as well as the best interest of those who have survived, to consider each missing teen as a rescue operation, but I honestly think it's unlikely that either of the two males not accounted for will get out of this alive."

"We don't know that Logan and Braydon didn't survive," I said, needing to believe we still had a chance with each of the teens. "Braydon was stabbed, but then he ran off. If no vital organs had been hit, he might have been able to stop the bleeding. If he managed to stop the bleeding, maybe he found a safe place to hang out while he healed." I took a deep breath. "At this point, we don't know what Braydon was wearing when the incident occurred or whether or not he had items on his person that would help him survive. The teens were backpacking in the Alaskan wilderness. It seems likely that they would have basic supplies such as a pocketknife and matches close at hand.

"Maybe, but I suspect they weren't prepared for a madman with a gun," Wyatt said.

"Maybe not," I admitted, although I knew in my gut that Braydon was likely dead given my previous vision which I felt certain had been of him. "But that doesn't mean that the teens didn't plan for other types of emergencies."

"And Logan?" Wyatt asked.

I shrugged. "Brit had no idea what happened to him. He was alive when the girls ran, but I get that being alive when last seen doesn't necessarily mean he's alive now. Still, I, for one, am going to continue to hold out hope."

Wyatt put an arm around my shoulder. "Yeah, me too. I know the odds aren't with us, but as long as there's a chance, there's a chance."

It took us a couple hours to reach the clearing Jake had identified as a place for Dani and Landon to meet up with us. Everyone was tired and thirsty, including the dogs, so we took a break while we waited for Dani to return. Jake had reached her on the radio just as they were leaving the airport, and she was happy to report that Carter had made it to the hospital. He hadn't regained consciousness, but his heart was beating, and he was breathing on his own, so that was something.

"Are you okay?" Houston asked me. I'd sat down on a log to take a break while we waited for Dani to arrive.

"I'm okay. Tired and a little headachy, but okay."
I reached out a hand to ruff Yukon's neck. "If we can
get to the four girls who are holed up in the cave
before something bad happens to one or more of
them, I think their rescue will go a long way toward
giving us all a second wind."

"I agree that finding the girls has to be our main
focus at this point."

"I'm going to try to connect with Brit while we
wait. The girls in the cave must be anxious for an
update. Dani seems to be taking longer to return than
I'd hoped, so letting Brit and the others know what is
going on seems to be a good idea."

"Okay. Do you need me to do anything?"

I held out my hand, and Houston laced his fingers
through mine. Once I had that link, I closed my eyes
and focused.

"Oh, good. I hoped you'd be back," Brit said,
connecting right away as if she had been waiting for
me. "Are you close?"

"We're getting there. We're waiting for the
chopper. We found Carter. He's alive."

"Oh, thank God."

I could sense that she was talking to the others. I
assumed to convey the good news about Carter. I
supposed that I should have told her that while he was
alive, he was near death, but for now, it seemed as if
it was best to give them some hope.

"So when will you get to us?" Brit asked after a moment.

"I'm not sure exactly. Dani, our pilot, took Carter to the hospital. She's on her way back now. Once she gets here, we'll set off again. How are the others?"

"Talia is good, and I think Carrie will be okay. She perked right up once she heard the news about Carter. But Alice is really sick. She's basically unconscious. I've been giving her sips of the water I collected after we spoke, but she's burning up, and when she does come to, she simply mumbles nonsense."

"Okay. Just stay where you are. Once Dani returns, I'm going to go up with her in the chopper. The crew and I saw a campfire earlier. We suspect it might have been the man who kidnapped you, although we don't know that for certain. If it was him, he's miles and miles away from the cave you're hiding in."

"I've been thinking it might be a good idea to get Alice outside. The cave is cold and damp, and the sunshine might do her good. Of course, if the fire you saw was not our kidnapper and he's still in the area, we run the risk of exposure."

"My instinct is that the kidnapper is likely miles away from where you're hiding. I can't guarantee this, however, so for now, maybe it would be best to stay where you are. It won't be much longer. I promise. Given the situation, I feel confident we'll be able to narrow things down enough to make our way to you before night falls again. Do you have matches?"

She paused and then answered. "Actually, yes. I have a fanny pack that I wear when I run. It was under my sweatshirt, so the kidnapper didn't know I had it and didn't take it. It has a pocketknife, a flare, matches, an emergency poncho that's small enough to fit in your pocket, and water tablets to purify water from a river or lake. I also have a collapsible cup. It's what I've been using to get water."

"Wow, that's great. If we get close enough but need to narrow in on your location more precisely, I may ask you to use that flare. For now, I think you should stay put. Once our group is underway again, I'll try to contact you with an update."

"Before you go. You said you found Carter. What about the others?"

"I'm afraid Pete is gone. I'm very, very sorry."

"I suspected as much. And the others?"

"So far, we haven't found either Braydon or Logan. Did Braydon and Logan have emergency supplies in their possession?"

"Braydon has a fanny pack like mine, but I can't remember if he had it on when he ran. He may have. He was bleeding, so unless he got help right away, I sort of doubt the outcome will be what we're hoping for. As for Logan, I can't remember if he had any supplies on him the last time I saw him, but he did have a knife, so maybe."

"Okay. I hear the chopper, so I have to go. I'm going to need to connect with you again, so try to stay open and listen for the echo of my voice in your head."

"I'll be listening," she promised.

Once Dani arrived, we all gathered to look at the map and discuss options. Dani should be able to get to the area in less than thirty minutes, but once she got there, she wouldn't be able to land. Given the thick umbrella of treetops, it was unlikely that she'd even be able to see anyone on the ground should there be someone to see. Those of us who would continue on foot had a long hike ahead, which would take hours from our current location.

"There has to be a meadow or field somewhere I can drop down on," Dani said.

"There likely is, but unless we can find such a place from the sky, it's going to be tough," Jake said.

"Trying to scout out a location and fly the bird at the same time is difficult. If someone wants to come up with me, perhaps we can find a way to drop the rescue party in closer."

"I'll go," I said. "On the one hand, part of me wants to stay on the ground to help the girls once we find them since I think Brit trusts me, and I feel like that trust is going to go a long way toward making the rescue go as smoothly as possible once we reach the teens. On the other hand, since I was able to view the area through Brit's eyes, I should be able to recognize landmarks as we narrowed down the search grid."

"If you want to go up, I can drop you in once we get close," Dani pointed out.

I glanced at Jake. "That makes sense. We'll need someone else to go up in the chopper with us to make sure the rope doesn't snag or tangle. One of the team members remaining on the ground will need to look after Yukon, but going with Dani as far as I can and then dropping in from the air does sound like the fastest way to get to Brit and the others."

Jake narrowed his gaze but ultimately agreed that if that was what I wanted to do, it was okay with him. Wyatt volunteered to go up with me to handle the rope I'd be tied to as it was lowered from the bird. We'd need to find a location without too much tree cover, but we wouldn't need as large of a space as we would should Dani attempt to land.

I remembered that when Brit had gone outside and turned in a circle, the cave she'd been hiding in had been behind her, Collins Glacier had been to her right, and Hallelujah Ridge had been in front of her. There had been trees all around her, but she'd heard a river she'd been unable to see. Based on these landmarks, we settled on a general location. I really wanted to narrow things down further before I was lowered to the ground since once I was in the middle of the tree cover, it would be difficult to make out the landmarks, so I settled in and connected with Brit. I asked her if she could hear the chopper. She said she did. I then asked her to go outside and set off her flare. It was a risk to do so if the kidnapper was still in the area, but it sounded as if Alice was in bad shape, and the need to get to her quickly seemed to outweigh an elevated sense of caution.

Once I had a specific GPS location as marked by the smoke from the flair, I marked it with my watch, and then Dani headed away from the trees toward an area where we felt it would be safe to use the rope. While looking for a place to rappel down, we noticed a ledge. It was narrow but flat and far enough away from the cliff face that drafts shouldn't be an issue. Dani was used to landing in dicey situations, so we changed our plans at the last minute, and rather than rappelling down, Dani set the bird on the ledge.

I climbed out, and Wyatt climbed out after me. Dani had a rescue board in the bird, so we took it with us. I had the GPS location where the flare was set off saved on my watch, so I used my compass to navigate the dense forest, hoping all the while that Alice would hold on just a bit longer.

"Oh my God, you found us," Brit cried, throwing herself into my arms once Wyatt and I arrived at the location where she'd been waiting for us.

"I told you I would." I hugged the girl as hard as I could. "Are the others still inside?"

She nodded.

"The chopper is about a mile from here. Dani will take all of you to the hospital."

Brit led us into the cave and showed us where the others were waiting. Carrie and Talia were weak but seemed okay and assured us they could walk to the chopper. Once Wyatt and I loaded Alice on the rescue board, we all set off toward the ledge where Dani was waiting. After we loaded everyone into the helicopter, Brit grabbed my arm. "What about Logan and Braydon?"

"We'll keep looking. You said that the last time you saw Braydon was at the campsite at Glacier Lake."

She nodded. "That man stabbed him, and Braydon took off running."

I couldn't help but remember the flash I'd seen of Braydon lying in a pool of blood. I figured there was no reason to bring that up now, so I assured Brit that we had officers from Fairbanks PD looking for him, and then I asked about Logan.

"I don't know what happened to him. He was alive when we ran, but Pete's dead, so maybe Logan is dead as well."

"Carter is alive," Carrie reminded her. "Maybe Logan got away."

"We'll find him," I said, even though I had no idea how we were going to do that. "Right now, Dani needs to get all of you to the hospital. I'll check in with you when I can."

After I hugged Brit one more time, I knocked on the door for Dani to take off. I supposed that I could have gone with them, but two teens were still missing, and as long as there were two teens missing, our job wasn't over.

Dani was able to radio Jake to let him know that she had the girls and that Wyatt and I were on our way back. We'd arranged to meet in a clearing at the foot of the ridge, which we'd initially identified as the location for Dani to land should we not find a closer place for me to rappel down. As I watched the sun begin its descent, I wondered if Logan and Braydon were alive or if we were simply wasting our time trying to find victims who were never going to be found.

By the time Wyatt and I had made it back to the clearing where we planned to meet up, regroup, and set up camp for the night, everyone was there. Houston shared that the officers from Fairbanks had finally found Braydon's body. It appeared that the teen had been able to travel on his own since his body was found almost two miles away from the campsite where he'd been injured, but his injuries had eventually been fatal. Dani had flown Braydon and the officers to Fairbanks.

I took a minute to mourn the quarterback who had worked hard to make his dream come true. Somehow, it seemed wrong that the impossible dream that had been so close to becoming a reality would never actually come to fruition. Braydon was an exceptional boy. His loss would be felt in the community in which he'd lived. I didn't know as much about Pete, but I was sure his death would be equally devastating. There was nothing I could do to undo what had been done. Carter was safe for now, so the only task before us was to find Logan and hopefully bring him home to those who loved and prayed for him.

"I figured all along that there was virtually no chance that Braydon would be found alive, but until you shared your news, I guess I never completely gave up hope," I said to Houston.

"I know what you mean. Braydon's death is going to hit the community hard."

"It's always hard to lose someone you were tasked with rescuing." I agreed.

Not that the rescue was a total failure. We'd set out to find eight teens, and so far, we'd lost two and rescued five. The two we lost were gone before we were even involved, but somehow it still felt like we'd failed. I know that sort of thinking was irrational, but it was hard when you were unable to bring everyone home. I still had no idea whether Carter and Alice would live, but the fact that we'd found them alive and given them a fighting chance at living meant a lot.

"So what now?" Landon asked after we'd all gathered by the fire to eat round two of the freeze-dried stew we had on hand.

"We look for Logan," I said.

"For how long?" Landon asked. "I don't mean to be insensitive, but we have no idea where to look for him."

"If he's dead, he'll likely be found within a mile of the location of the showdown where the girls got away after Carter was stabbed," Wyatt pointed out. "It makes the most sense to head back to that location to begin the search. If Logan's alive and left the area under his own power, then he started off from there."

"The fire we saw was north of the location I've begun to think of as ground zero," Jake said. "And I agree that it makes sense that we head in that direction. A well-groomed hiking trail runs through the area. If Logan ran mindlessly, unsure of a direction, he might have followed the trail had he run across it at some point."

"It's been days," Landon pointed out. "That boy is likely dead."

"Likely? Yes," I said. "Certainly? No. We have to keep looking until we know for certain one way or another."

"We don't always find those we're tasked with finding," Jake reminded us.

Jake was right. We had never found Val, yet, even for her, we eventually stopped looking. In my opinion, we hadn't looked for Logan hardly at all. At least not individually. I'd been connected with Brit, and finding her and the other girls had been our priority. The officers from Fairbanks had been tasked with finding Braydon, and we'd simply stumbled upon Pete and Carter. The least we could do was make Logan our focus and priority for a day or two before giving up completely.

"We're all exhausted," Houston said. "I think we should get some sleep and then develop a plan in the morning."

"I think we should go back to the last place Logan was seen, which was the clearing where the boys decided to take a stand. Maybe the dogs will be able to pick up a scent, or maybe they won't, but we at least need to try," I said.

In theory, everyone agreed with my assessment of the situation. It did make sense to return to the last location where we knew Logan was alive. I could tell the entire team was beginning to feel the effects of being out in the elements without a break. In my mind, going home without Logan simply wasn't an option, but if we didn't pick up a new lead the following day, I suspected returning to Rescue might be the only option that made sense.

Chapter 7

"Coffee," Houston handed me a mug of steaming hot coffee the following morning.

I slowly opened my eyes, trying all the while to figure out why Houston was in my bedroom. It took me a minute, but I eventually remembered that I was in a tent, not in my bedroom. "What time is it?"

"Eight o'clock. The entire team was exhausted, including the dogs, so Jake decided to let everyone sleep in a bit."

I had to admire the way Houston seemed to willingly defer to Jake running things and making the decisions. I supposed that since two people had died and our search had gone from a simple rescue to a murder investigation, Houston had every right to claim jurisdiction, but he hadn't. Part of me wondered why and part of me was just happy that he worked so well with the team.

"I need to call Harley before we head out," I said. "I should be able to get service with my satellite phone from the clearing unless the mountain range between here and Rescue interferes."

"I called my office earlier to check in, and I got through fine," Houston informed me. "You'll be happy to know that Carter is awake, and while he's still considered to be in critical condition, he's stable for now."

"And Alice?"

"Doing much better as well."

I smiled, but then I remembered the teens who hadn't made it. "I guess the parents of Braydon and Pete have been notified."

Houston nodded. "I spoke to the coroner. It seems that Pete went quickly, but Braydon actually hung on for a while. Not long enough that we had any chance of reaching him on time. Even without the injury he suffered, it's unlikely he would have survived very long without supplies."

"I think I might have connected with him briefly that first day at the campsite. I experienced a flash of an image of him lying on the ground."

"If you connected with him, wouldn't you be looking at things through his eyes rather than looking at him from above?" Houston asked.

I frowned. "Actually, you make a good point. I wouldn't have been viewing the scene from above if I'd connected with Braydon, so I guess I must have been connecting with someone who came across the body. But who?"

"Perhaps the killer."

Now that was a sobering thought. Had the killer returned to the first campsite he'd destroyed after the girls had gotten away? Or had it been Logan? Of course, if Logan had found his way back to that first campsite, he should have been able to easily hike the rest of the way out. The fact that he didn't find his way out suggested that he was dead, seriously injured, or disoriented and heading in the wrong direction. I hoped for the latter, but at this point, I actually suspected the first option presented.

"I'm going to make a few more calls," Houston announced. "There's food on the fire and plenty of coffee, so it's best to fill up before we head out."

"Thanks for the coffee. I'll grab a bite to eat once I've called Harley."

Houston nodded and left. It was hard to describe our relationship. We were friends for sure. Good friends who seemed to have been heading toward something more at one point, but that something more seemed to have stalled even before the kidnapping fiasco. Still, despite everything that had occurred, or more precisely, had not occurred, there was this feeling that we were on the cusp of something more. Houston had been recently divorced when he'd moved to Alaska, so I understood his reluctance to get into a relationship with anyone so soon after ending one, but it had been years, and it seemed like he'd be over the fallout created by the end of his marriage by this point. And he had shown some interest, at least in the beginning. I'd noticed a cooling, but he'd never mentioned a particular reason for the cooling. Of course, given my visions, nightmares, and tendency to get those around me into life-and-death situations, I wasn't an easy person to have a relationship with.

"Hey, Harley," I said, stifling a yawn once my call had gone through.

"Harm, are you okay? I've been picking up random bits of news via the gossip hotline, but I'm pretty sure I don't have the whole story."

"I'm fine. Everyone from the team is fine. So far, we've found all but one of the missing teens."

"Alive?" he asked.

"Five are alive; two didn't make it. I wish I could say I was on my way back, but since we still have one missing teen, the team has decided to stay out here another day or two in an attempt to find him."

"I understand. And don't worry about your animals. Serena has been staying at your place overnight, and I've been going over every day to help with the exercise and chores. We're fine, so you don't need to worry about anything and can focus on doing what you need to do."

"Thanks, Harley. It means a lot that you're both there, and I don't have to worry about things at home. How are things at the shelter?"

"Everything is good. We had a litter of husky puppies dropped off yesterday. They're healthy and almost old enough to be rehomed, but the owner of the mama dog was being transferred and couldn't hang around long enough to get them adopted. I think they'll go fast once we make them available. Kelly has given them their shots and a clean bill of health, so we'll likely start taking applications." Harley referred to the local veterinarian, Kelly Austin.

"We tend to get a lot of puppies and kittens at this time of the year, so beginning the application process now is a good idea. In fact, when I get back, we should sit down and discuss the idea of having an adoption clinic."

"I plan to be around for the rest of the year, so I'm on board to help. Maybe we can even do a fundraiser of some sort."

"That would be helpful. What sort of timeline are we looking at? Have you signed on for another movie?"

"No. I have scripts for a couple movies that will film early next year. I'll probably do something next winter after the holidays, but I'd like to free up my schedule a bit, and I've spoken to my agent about keeping my commitment to one movie a year."

"That'd be great. You know we all miss you when you're gone."

"And I miss everyone here. I'm going to try making Rescue my primary home and see how that goes. If things go as I hope, I'll be in Rescue for seven or eight months out of every twelve."

"That'd be awesome. Since you're going to be around more, maybe we can do another concert in the fall. The last concert raised enough money to buy food and supplies for the entire winter."

"I think I can arrange something. We'll use my estate again. There was plenty of room for parking, and the turnout was even better than I'd hoped. I can start reaching out to some of my friends in the music industry. I think it will be fun."

"That would be fantastic." I glanced at the sun, which was already climbing into the sky. "Listen, I really need to go. I'll try to check in at the end of the day so that you have an actual update and not just gossip to rely on. And tell Serena thanks. I'll try to call her later as well."

After I hung up, I headed toward the fire where most of the team had gathered. Jake had talked to Sarge, who'd been researching a missing person named Hope. It was our theory that the killer had suffered the loss of someone in his life with that name and, as a result of that loss, had suffered a psychotic break. The fact that this man was wandering around the Alaskan wilderness looking for someone named Hope suggested to us that if we could figure out who Hope was, then maybe we could figure out the identity of our killer.

"So far, Sarge has only found one missing person named Hope," Jake informed us. "Hope Sullivan was a fourteen-year-old who became lost during a camping trip with her father twelve years ago. There was an exhaustive search, but she was never found. At some point, the search was called off, but the girl's father refused to stop looking. There were reports of him wandering this wilderness from the first snowmelt in the spring until it fell again in the fall for years after the event. I haven't heard anything more about it personally, but Sarge found reports called in by hikers in the area reporting that there was a man with crazy eyes wandering the area looking for the daughter he lost all those years ago."

"So he's been looking for his daughter for twelve years?" I asked.

"That would seem to be the case for a while; however, Sarge couldn't find any reports for the past several years. During the first half dozen years after the girl went missing, there were reports from hikers every summer, but the sightings seemed to have stopped after five or six years until last summer, when a couple teens from a church group reported that they'd come across a man who seemed to be wandering aimlessly, looking for someone named Hope."

"So something must have set him off recently," Landon said.

"Based on what we know, that seems to be as good a guess as any," Jake agreed. "While the man was disorganized and delusional, he never seemed dangerous in the past, so if it is the same man, I'm not sure what changed."

"Maybe someone tried to help by telling him about a young woman they'd seen while hiking, and that fueled his fantasy of finding his daughter," Wyatt said.

"Yeah, but why did he kill those teens?" Landon asked.

"Grief has a way of eating at your mind and your soul over time until all that's left of the person you once were is a memory," Houston said. "If this man has been actively looking for his daughter all this time, that means he never gave up. He never found a way to find peace. He's likely been living in his own hell for a dozen years. That sort of torment can go a long way toward destroying a person's mind and sanity."

I had to admit that if our killer was this grieving father, I felt sadness for the man. Not that grieving justified what he'd done to the teens we'd been called out to find, but I supposed the story Jake told at least explained things.

"So, how does knowing this help us to know where to look next?" Wyatt asked.

"Maybe the man is traveling a route year after year," Houston suggested. "It would help if we knew where the sightings occurred."

"I'll have Sarge look into it," Jake said. "The reports of a man stopping hikers to ask about Hope go back to that first summer, so perhaps we will be able to determine whether or not the man is sticking to a specific route."

"Brit told me that after the man tied them up and made them go with him, they just wandered aimlessly for days," I shared.

"One man's aimless is another man's plan," Houston said. "At this point, all we really have is the last place Logan was seen alive. I say we check that out and try to pick up a trail."

Houston's plan seemed to be the only viable option we had, so we set off in that direction. As we hiked, we discussed the situation. The idea that the person whose eyes I'd seen Braydon laying on the ground through likely didn't belong to anyone in the group had thrown me a bit. By the time we'd reached the campsite, and I'd had the vision of Braydon, the group of friends had already separated, the girls were already hiding, Pete was already dead, and Carter was likely already unconscious. If a random hiker had come across the body, it seemed to me that he or she would have called it in, which likely meant that it was the killer I'd connected with. But if it was the killer, why come back to the campsite? If it was the killer, what had he hoped to accomplish by returning to the scene of the crime? Perhaps he thought the girls had returned to the first campsite to gather their things after they'd run off, and he was there looking for them. In a way, that theory actually made sense. I wasn't sure how I could know whose eyes I'd witnessed Braydon's body through, but it had been days, so if it was the killer, he was most likely long gone by this point.

Jake had announced that we'd stop to take a short break before we passed the fork in the trail that led to the back of the crater. I wanted to call Brit since reception would be dicey once we headed around to the back of the tall mountain peak. I wondered how the group was doing. I hoped Carter and Alice would recover, and I hoped that those we'd managed to rescue would find a way to deal with the loss of their friends and overcome the horror they'd endured without ruining their lives and sanity.

Chapter 8

"Harmony, is that you?" Brit asked several hours later. The team had stopped to rest and hydrate, and I'd used that time to make my call.

"It's me," I verified.

"The service is bad. I can barely hear you. Are you okay?" Brit asked.

"I'm fine. We're in an area with a lot of mountains, which interferes with the signal."

"Have you found Logan?"

"Not yet, but we're still looking. Do you have any idea which direction Logan might have gone if he'd managed to get free of his captor?"

"I don't know this for a fact, but I think he would have headed back to the parking area where we'd left the vehicles. Logan's only lived in Alaska for a few years, and he mentioned that he didn't have a lot of backpacking experience and wasn't familiar with the area. The only reason he was even with us is because Braydon invited him."

"So, Logan hadn't been planning to attend from the beginning?" I asked.

"No. In the beginning, it was just going to be Braydon and me, but then Braydon told Pete and Carter about our plans, and both boys decided to come with us. Carter invited Carrie, and I thought it would just be the five of us. When Logan somehow found out about the trip, Braydon asked if he'd like to join us, which he did, and then he invited Talia and Alice."

"So, how do you and Braydon know each other?" Not that knowing was essential at this point, but I was curious.

"Braydon and I go way back. Not as a couple but as friends. We're both athletic, and we've hiked and run together in the past." Brit paused and then continued. "I really hope you find Logan alive, but I won't be surprised if you don't. It's been days, and Logan doesn't strike me as the type who could survive for days on his own in the wilderness."

"Have you spoken to the others?" I asked.

"My mom is keeping me close to home, but I spoke to Carrie on the phone. She's doing better. Carter is still in the hospital, but he's doing better as well, and I heard that Alice has been downgraded from critical condition to stable, and everyone I've spoken to thinks she'll be fine."

"And Talia?"

"I haven't spoken to her, but she seemed fine the whole time. I think she may have gone back to California."

I turned and looked to where the others were waiting. "I need to go. The team is only taking a short break, and I need to grab some water and maybe a granola bar. I'm not sure if I'll be able to check in with you this evening, but I'll try. If not this evening, then tomorrow."

"Thanks, Harmony. I do appreciate the updates. It's literally killing me that Braydon and Pete are gone. I really do hope you can find Logan before it's too late."

After I rejoined the team, we decided to head toward the location at the back of Aloha Lake, where Brit had told us that Logan and Carter had taken a stand. It was on the way to the area where we'd seen the campfire, so it made sense to take a closer look. We figured we'd allow the dogs to search the area thoroughly, and if they didn't find Logan, we'd head toward the location of the campfire we'd seen from the top of the mountain. If there still was no sign of the teen and the dogs hadn't picked up a scent, we'd likely turn around and head back toward the trailhead. The Alaskan wilderness was massive, and we couldn't search every inch of it looking for a single teen unless we could pick up something that would point us in a direction.

Once we reached our first destination at the back of Aloha Lake, I'd try to connect with Logan again, but so far, my attempts had all met with complete failure. Either the teen was unconscious or dead, or he could feel my presence and was intentionally blocking me. At this point, I really had no idea which scenario was accurate.

"Have you picked up anything that would suggest this isn't a total waste of time?" Landon asked as he fell in beside Yukon and me as we hiked.

"No, if Logan is alive, he's either blocking me or simply not susceptible to my presence in his mind."

"What about trying to connect with the killer," Landon suggested. "You've done it before."

I had done it before. I'd hated every minute I spent in the mind of the deranged individuals I'd chosen to connect with, but it was an ability I'd experienced some success with in the past.

"You can ask Brit for a description," Landon continued when I didn't answer right away. "She seemed to have survived the ordeal in one piece, and given the conversations you've had to this point, she seems willing to help."

I really wanted to say no to this suggestion. It already felt as if my head was going to explode, but I supposed that if I was able to connect with the killer, I might be able to determine where he was currently camping and what his next move might be. I wasn't sure that connecting with the man would help us find Logan, but I supposed it couldn't hurt to see if I could get a glimpse of what he knew. "Okay," I said. "I'll see if I can get Brit and Sarge together. Sarge has a photo of the father of the child we suspect the killer is looking for, and Brit has seen the killer. If Brit can confirm that the man Sarge believes may be our killer actually is our killer, they can forward me a photo to work from."

"There's a clearing up ahead where we stopped that first day. Let's take a break, and you can make your calls to both Brit and Sarge. Once you hook the two of them up with each other, I guess we can continue on."

Jake and Houston both liked Landon's plan, so that's what we did. It was late in the day, although still daylight by the time we reached the location where Carter and Logan had confronted the killer, so we decided to set up camp. I'd called and spoken to Brit earlier, while Jake had called and spoken to Sarge. They planned to speak to each other, and I hoped to get through to Brit again once we'd stopped hiking for the day.

"Any luck finding Logan?" Brit asked once I'd set up my tent and made my call.

"Not yet. How did things go with Sarge?"

"Good. The photo Sarge has of the father of the missing teenager is old. In the photo, the man is clear-eyed and clean-cut, whereas the man who kidnapped us has a full beard, long greasy hair, and a crazed look in his eyes, which I believe actually changed the color of his eyes from their original gray, assuming, of course, that the man in the photo is the kidnapper. I really tried to look past the changes, but the best I could tell Sarge is that it's possible that the two men could be one and the same, but I just couldn't be sure."

"That's understandable. The photo Sarge was able to dig up is at least a decade old, and if the man went from clean-shaven to a full beard, that has to make a huge difference.

"The fact that both men seem to be looking for someone named Hope makes it seem as if the man in the photo could be the same man who kidnapped us and killed Braydon and Pete. I think Sarge plans to send both the photo from a decade ago and the drawing I was able to sketch of the man I remember to Jake. I hope this helps you connect with this man. I hope that by connecting, you can find Logan."

"I hope so too."

Brit seemed to pause thoughtfully before speaking again. "Is it really awful to get inside the head of a crazy person?"

"It isn't fun."

"I figure there must be so much pain and anger inside this man to cause him to act the way he has. Not that I'm even close to forgiving him, but after I spoke to Sarge and we looked back at everything the man has been through in his attempt to find his missing child, I guess I can sort of see how, given enough time, that might make a person crazy."

"I'm sure the pain of not having answers about your child's fate is enough to make anyone crazy."

After I hung up with Brit, I called Serena. I'd spoken to Harley a couple times, but I hadn't spoken to Serena since this whole thing had started. Harley said that Serena was spending the night in my cabin. I wondered how she was doing with Denali. I wouldn't be at all surprised if she told me that he'd decided that I'd been gone long enough and had wandered off to find me.

"All the animals are doing fine, but you aren't wrong about Denali," Serena informed me after she answered my call. "He hasn't wandered off, but he won't come in. He just lays out there on the front porch waiting for you. Every now and again, he'll take a lap around the property, and he seems friendly when I go outside to feed him or to take care of the animals in the barn, but he won't come inside and relax with the other animals."

"His behavior isn't surprising, and as long as he's eating, drinking, and staying close to home, I guess we won't bother him. I hope to be home in a couple days. Let me know if things escalate between now and then, and I'll have Dani bring me back. Denali isn't the sort of dog you can make do anything unless he wants to do it anyway."

"He seems okay as long as I don't try to force him inside," Serena said. "Harley came by yesterday, and we took all the dogs for a long walk to the lake. Denali looked hesitant at first, but he eventually came along with us. He seemed extra alert, but I suppose he was looking for you along the trail."

"How are the other dogs doing?"

"They're fine. Honey misses you. She slept right next to me last night, but she seems to be fine. Shia is her normal funny, playful self, and Lucky is as chill and laid back as he always is. I noticed Kodi was limping after our walk, so I called Kelly. She said that he was getting old and it was likely that he had just overdone it, and suggested that both he and Juno take it easy today. Harley and I talked about it and decided that instead of taking a long walk, we'd just play with the dogs in the yard. We weren't sure we could convince Denali to come with us again anyway."

"That sounds like a good idea. Are the cats all doing okay?"

"Moose has been moody, but I suppose that's normal. The other cats seem fine. Did Harley tell you about the husky puppies who were surrendered to the shelter? I brought one by yesterday to see how she did with the other animals, which made Moose mad, but overall, I'd say the experiment was successful."

"The dogs, other than Denali, are pretty chill, and the cats, other than Moose, seem to go with the flow. Any particular reason you decided to bring one of the pups over?"

"I've been thinking about adopting a pet, and these pups are just so cute. I guess I just wanted to see how the pup, who caught my eye, would do with other animals. Of course, there are a bunch of animals at the shelter I could have exposed her to, but I was locking up to come over here, and she was just staring at me, so I decided to bring her."

"A dog is a wonderful companion. To be honest, I'm surprised you don't have a houseful already. You're obviously a dog person."

"I am a dog person and a cat person and an all kinds of an animal person, but I guess I've just had it in the back of my mind that I might want to travel before taking on such a responsibility, but things have changed. I feel more of a commitment to be here now, and I can see myself staying close to home in the immediate future. If I'm going to be here in Rescue for the long haul and not chasing adventures, then maybe I will adopt a pet."

I knew that the thing that had changed for Serena was Harley Medford. She had it bad for him, but I wasn't sure how things would work out in the long run since he had never been the sort who wanted to be tied down to anyone. Serena and Harley got along very well, and they both loved Rescue and animals, so maybe they could find a way to make it work. In the past, Harley was out of town more often than he was in town, which made it impossible for him to cultivate a relationship. Maybe Harley and Serena could find their way toward each other if Harley started spending the majority of his time in Alaska as he kept threatening to.

After I hung up with Serena, I joined the others by the fire. Everyone, other than Dani, who was back in Rescue awaiting additional instructions, had gathered.

"Are you ready?" Jake asked me.

I nodded. The idea of having to intentionally connect with the killer was causing me all sorts of anxiety. The plan to do so was a good one. In fact, it was the only plan we had at this point, but based on experience, I knew that connecting with these sorts of individuals would eat away at my soul a little at a time. After my last go-around with a killer who liked to play games at the expense of my friends, I honestly feared that I'd been changed forever. During those first days after Houston left, I had found myself imagining a pile of ashes and the memory of the person I'd been before I'd allowed my mind to be mired in so much darkness.

"I know what this does to you, so only go as far as you feel comfortable going," he cautioned. "I really want to find Logan, and it would be great if we could track down the killer and bring him to justice, but I don't want to lose you in the process."

"I'll be fine," I assured him. "If this man has gone from a grieving father to a cold-blooded killer, we need to find him. We know he's responsible for two deaths, and it seems likely that he might very well kill again."

The guys had set up a tent while I was on the phone, so I decided that was the best place to work. I could find privacy and a bit of seclusion, both of which were necessary in order to make this type of connection. Jake volunteered to act as my anchor, but Houston volunteered as well. I decided to have Houston help me this time. Jake had always been there for me in the past, and I knew he'd be there for me in the future, but somehow, I felt it was important for Houston and me to regain the connection we'd had before the incident that had almost torn us apart permanently.

"If you need me to do anything specific, just let me know," Houston said.

"I will. I'm going to lie down. I just want you to hold my hands and sit quietly with me. If I say something, try to pay attention to what I say, but don't interrupt."

"Okay. I'm ready whenever you are."

I closed my eyes and focused on the man in the photo Sarge had found. I also allowed room in my mind for the sketch Brit had created. The two images wouldn't merge in my mind, and at this point, I felt less than confident that the man who'd been looking for his daughter and the killer were one and the same. Still, it would be just too odd if they weren't. What were the odds there would be two men wandering around in the same wilderness area looking for someone named Hope?

I tried to focus in on the man in the sketch since we knew he was the killer. I opened my mind and tried to find the voice in his head that would help me to connect with his thoughts and motivations. After thirty minutes, I realized that a connection was not in my immediate future. I was about to open my eyes when I saw the same flash of Braydon lying on his stomach in a pool of blood I'd seen before. Braydon's body had been recovered, so the image had to have been a memory. But who's memory? The killers? It had been the killer I'd been aiming for, so the idea that the killer had backtracked and found Braydon's body after Braydon had passed did make a lot of sense. I thought of the man with the full beard, long greasy hair, and dead eyes. I tried with all my might to find my way into his mind. If I could connect with his memories, then maybe I could connect in real time. If I could see what he saw, then perhaps I'd see enough to allow us to track this man and hopefully find Logan.

Chapter 9

"While I always enjoy spending time in the wilderness, I am to that point where I'd kill for a big juicy burger or a steak with all the trimmings," Wyatt said. "Do we have a plan for going forward? I know that we'd all like to find both Logan and the killer, but I'm just not sure how we're going to accomplish that if Harmony isn't able to connect with one or the other or we don't pick up a trail."

"Wyatt's right," Landon said. "We can't just wander aimlessly."

Jake looked toward Houston. "What do you think? Do we call it a day, or do we keep going?"

He hesitated for just a beat before responding. "If Harmony doesn't pick up anything that will help us track these men down, and nothing else happens between now and morning to provide a direction for us to look, then I guess I'll have to vote with the others to call it. I really hate doing that, but at this point, aimlessly wondering is getting us nowhere."

"I'll try to connect with either Logan or the killer again before I turn in," I said. "I'm not sure I'll be any more successful than I've been to this point, but I won't feel good about quitting unless I know I've done everything I possibly can."

"I'm not going to talk you out of trying again since I think that connecting with either Logan or the killer is the only hope we have of finding either man, but I do want you to be careful," Jake said. "You look pale, and I suspect your head feels as if it is about to explode."

An explosion might help to relieve the pressure, but I didn't say as much. Complaining about my head wouldn't help, and I knew that if the guys realized how much pain I was in, they'd probably try to talk me out of doing what I knew I needed to do.

At some point, Houston must have realized that it would be helpful for me to focus on something else for a while, so he changed the subject. If not for the fact that a man was missing and teens had died, I might have actually enjoyed the next couple of hours sitting around a campfire and chatting with my friends as the summer sky slowly began to darken. We talked about the new equipment Jake had bought for the team, which hadn't been delivered yet, but he was hoping everything would arrive in the next couple of weeks. The thing about rescue equipment is that you never want to have to use it, while at the same time, there's a part of you that can't wait to try it out.

I glanced across the fire where Yukon, Sitka, and Kojak were sleeping in a pile. The dogs had worked hard since the moment we arrived at the trailhead, and while they hadn't been directly responsible for any finds on this trip, they'd been "on duty" the entire time, and I knew they'd appreciate a few days off as well.

Once the bright sky had turned to twilight, I crawled back into the tent I'd been sharing with Houston and closed my eyes. By this point, I was so tired that I suspected that if I didn't connect right away, I'd likely fall asleep, and just as I was about to drift off into an exhaustion-induced slumber, I caught a glimpse of the darkening landscape through someone's eyes. I wasn't sure if the someone was Logan or the killer, but it didn't really matter at this point. We had a new direction and a new clue to chase down.

"I could see a lake. There was a tent next to the lake, and between the tent and the lake, there was a firepit that was dormant but showed evidence of recent use."

"Was this campsite anywhere near the smoke we saw on that first day?" Houston asked.

"It was. I suspect the campsite I saw in my vision is the same campsite the smoke came from."

"And you have no idea whose eyes you were looking through?" Houston asked.

I slowly shook my head. "No, I was focusing on the killer, but I didn't feel the same rage and darkness I've felt when connecting with killers in the past. It could have been Logan had he survived. But Logan didn't have a tent or any supplies when he ran, so if the person I connected with was Logan, I'm not sure where he got the supplies I noticed in the vision. And then there's the possibility that I connected with a random camper, and my vision had nothing to do with either Logan or the killer. That's unlikely but not impossible, especially if the person camping by the lake is in some sort of physical or emotional pain."

"Okay," Houston said. "Get some sleep. I can't tell the others what to do, but given your vision, I'm going to head to the campsite by the lake at first light. Someone is still hanging around over there. If it's a camper, he may be in distress of some sort. If it's Logan, then he's in need of rescue. And if it's the killer, then we might be able to catch this guy before he can hurt anyone else."

Chapter 10

First light came early at this time of the year. Houston had spoken to the team, and everyone agreed to head toward the campsite that had been identified initially by smoke and then confirmed by my vision to still be occupied. Based on our best estimate, it would take about half a day to get there and then a day and a half to hike back to the parking area. And that was if we really hurried and didn't stop to take a lot of breaks. The reality was that we were likely to be looking at another two nights in the wilderness, at the very least. Jake asked everyone for a status on the supplies they carried. If there was one thing that you never wanted to do, it was to hike into the wilderness without everything you'd need to face any emergency or situation. With the crater being between us and the campsite we were heading toward, we weren't going to be traveling across the sort of terrain that would allow Dani to bail us out should we end up in trouble.

As we neared the campsite, which we'd pinned to our GPS map based on our best estimate of where it was located, Houston called us all to a stop. Since we didn't know who I'd connected with and really had no idea whether we'd be met with a heartfelt welcome or a rain of gunfire, Houston suggested that we proceed slowly. His plan was to access the area on his own and assess the situation before we attempted to enter the camping area as a group. I wasn't a fan of Houston approaching the campsite on his own, but he was the cop, and given the intensity of the situation, I think we all realized that it was time for him to take the reins and begin making decisions for the group.

All three dogs stayed with Wyatt, Landon, and me while Houston continued forward. Jake took up a position slightly behind him. Both men knew what they were doing, and both men had guns, so I decided to wait where I was told, allowing Jake and Houston to do what it was they'd been trained to do.

"Do you have any idea who you were connected with when you observed this campsite?" Landon asked.

I slowly shook my head. "I normally have access to what the person I'm connected with is feeling, but all I had this time was a flash of a vision of what the individual was seeing, but not what they were feeling. I have no idea what Jake and Houston are going to find." I looked down at my radio. The men were supposed to let us know if they needed backup. They also planned to let us know if it was safe to join them once they arrived at the campsite and evaluated the situation.

"Shouldn't they have been there by now?" I asked the others, even though it really hadn't been all that long since the men had faded into the forest.

"I'm sure they're taking it slow, so they don't attract any attention until they can figure out what we're dealing with," Wyatt answered. "If we don't hear from them in another twenty minutes, one of us will go to check on the situation."

Luckily, Jake radioed fifteen minutes later and let us know that the man camping at the lakeside campsite had been there for a week and was neither the killer nor Logan. He said that the camper had had a visit from a man fitting the killer's description late the previous day. He confirmed that the visitor had been looking for a girl named Hope. The camper also reported that the man had seemed completely out of his mind. He'd wanted to get rid of the visitor and told the man that he'd seen a girl fitting the description he'd provided camping over the ridge at Aloha Lake.

"So I must have briefly connected to the killer while he was talking to the man who has been staying at the campsite all week," I said. "That's the only reason I can think of why I would have seen what I saw when I tried to connect with the killer last night." I frowned. "It is odd, however, that I couldn't feel what the killer was feeling. I usually can."

"It was a brief encounter, and if you happened to connect just as the killer was talking to the man he'd come across camping by the lake, the killer was likely distracted. He may not have been experiencing mental distress at that moment," Landon said.

I supposed that could be what had occurred. Jake had instructed Wyatt, Landon, and me to wait where we were, so we did as he asked. By the time Jake and Houston made their way back to us, it was past time for lunch, so we decided to take a break and reassess the situation.

"So what now?" Landon asked after we'd found a good spot to take a break. "The hike down into the crater to access Aloha Lake is long and strenuous. If the killer went down into the crater looking for Hope, and if he is still there, which is unlikely, then the effort might be worth it. But if the killer was never there, or if he was there, but has since left, then we'd be wasting an entire day making the trek down."

It was apparent to me that everyone was tired. It wasn't as if we'd been engaged in a relaxing backpacking trip. We'd been walking almost continuously and existing on freeze-dried food and very little sleep on top of that. After a bit of discussion, we decided to head back to Rescue and get some rest. It was extremely unlikely that Logan was still alive. Even if he hadn't been injured by the killer, it had been days since the showdown, and according to Brit, Logan hadn't had the supplies or knowledge one would need to survive in the wilderness for days at a time.

"Let's head back," Jake said. "We all need to refuel mentally and physically. Once we have a chance to rest up, we'll regroup and see if we can figure out a different way of approaching things."

The hike back toward the parking area seemed endless. When we reached Glacier Lake and the campsite where the killer had first run into the teens, Jake suggested we break for the night. Based on its proximity to water and the trail, which would take us back to the parking area, it was a good place to stop, but it felt somewhat spooky now that I knew that Braydon had died not all that far from here. Still, his body had been removed, and it didn't make sense to look for another flat area large enough for three tents with access to both water and a firepit. I figured we'd only be here for a few hours before it got light again, and then we'd want to continue on our way. The chit-chat around the fire was kept to a minimum as everyone fueled and then headed to the tents to get some shut-eye. I fell asleep the minute my head touched the ground and would likely have slept clear through to the following day had nature not called.

"What is it?" Houston asked, sitting up.

"I need to use the facilities," I said, pulling my shoes and jacket on and grabbing my gun. "I'll just be a minute."

"I'll come with you."

I gave him a look that I hoped conveyed my lack of enthusiasm for his suggestion.

"I'll give you some space, but you shouldn't be out there alone."

"Okay," I finally agreed. "But once I find a spot to take care of things, you have to promise to keep your back turned."

"I will. I promise."

If Yukon had been sleeping in our tent instead of with the other dogs in Jake's tent, I could have just brought him with me as a lookout.

I'd noticed a natural wall made from rocks when I'd gone looking for a place earlier, so I headed in that direction. I'd just squatted when I heard a rustling beyond the wall where Houston was waiting. "Is everything okay?" I asked as I stood and buttoned my pants.

When he didn't answer right away, I bent over to pick up my gun.

"Don't make a sound or move, or your friend will die."

Chapter 11

In retrospect, I should have chosen a spot closer to the campsite to take care of nature's call. If Houston and I had been closer to the other tents, then chances were that the dogs would have heard the commotion and would have alerted the others to our predicament. I'd considered screaming, but the man with the full beard and long greasy hair was holding a gun to Houston's head. He told me he'd kill him if I made a sound, and I believed him. The man handed me a roll of duct tape, and when he told me to put a strip over Houston's mouth, I did. When he told me to put a strip over my mouth, I did that as well. The man tied a rope to each of our wrists, which he then tied to his backpack. Once he was convinced we were secure and unlikely to cause him trouble, he began to walk. I hoped someone would wake up and hear us, but everyone was exhausted, and it was unlikely that anyone would even know we were missing until the sun came up and someone came to our tent to wake us. I'd connected with Jake in the past and hoped I could do so again, but the reality was that his mind wouldn't be receptive until he woke up.

The direction we headed was due south, which was a direction we hadn't attempted during our search for the teens who'd been kidnapped. I knew that leaving a trail for the dogs to follow was essential, so as soon as the man turned his back, I reached my hand up to my head and pulled out a couple hairs, which I then allowed to float to the ground. I repeated the movement every few steps. My hair was long and quite thick, so it was unlikely I'd run out anytime soon, but I did hope that someone from our campsite would wake up and realize we were missing before we got too far away since that would make us harder to find.

After we'd been walking for about two hours, our kidnapper stopped. He motioned for us to sit down, and once we had done so, he pulled the tape from our mouths and gave us each a drink of water. He must have figured that we were far enough from our campsite that there wasn't a risk of being heard since he simply slid his backpack off and sat down next to it instead of replacing the tape.

"Where are you taking us?" I asked.

He ignored me.

"Is there something we can do to help you? Are you the man who's looking for Hope?"

He continued to ignore us.

"Maybe I can help you." I glanced at Houston. "Maybe we both can. If you untie us, Houston and I will help you look for her."

He didn't turn and look at us or speak or respond in any way. I almost wondered if the man was deaf. He'd spoken when he captured us, so I knew the man could speak if he chose to. The way he totally ignored everything I'd said was actually pretty creepy. I could see why the teens had thought they could make a move. They probably thought that since he wasn't the sort to speak, that meant he wasn't paying attention.

I wasn't sure how long our break would last, so I decided to look around. It was light but just barely. There was a good chance that the gang was beginning to rise, but there was an equal chance that everyone had slept in a bit since we only had a seven-hour hike ahead of us. I knew it would be hard to make a connection with Jake while we were walking, so I took a chance and closed my eyes.

"Jake, are you there? It's Harmony."

I waited for a minute and tried again.

"Jake, can you hear me?"

Again, I waited. If Jake didn't realize that I was missing, he wouldn't be listening for me, and that would make it much harder for me to get through to him.

"Jake, I need you to hear me. It's Harm. Are you awake?"

I paused to wait for a reply that didn't come.

"Wake up, Jake!"

While I didn't suppose it was possible to scream in your mind, the sound in my head was quite loud.

"Harm?" Jake asked. "Where are you? What's going on?"

"The man who took the teens kidnapped Houston and me last night. We've been hiking for about three hours. We're heading south."

I was about to look around and offer additional details when the man who'd kidnapped us stood up and pulled Houston and me to our feet. That broke the connection between Jake and me. At least for now. I knew that Jake was likely looking in our tent right about now to confirm what he thought he'd heard in his mind. Once he did, he'd wake everyone who wasn't already awake, and the search would be on. I suspected he'd call Dani to bring the bird, but that would take at least an hour. Probably longer.

As we walked, I tried to connect with Jake again, but the terrain had grown steep, and I was so busy trying to keep myself from falling on the loose shale that I found it impossible to concentrate. I couldn't imagine why this man had taken Houston and me in the first place. If he was looking for someone, it seemed that dragging hostages along would only slow him down. When I stopped to really think about it, I realized that it had made no sense for him to have dragged the teens along when he did. I had to wonder what his long-range plan was. Was he going to kill us? If so, why not just do it and get it over with. Thinking back, while the man had stabbed three people, he hadn't acted in a violent manner until his victims attacked him when they tried to escape. I supposed that bode well for Houston and me. It likely meant that as long as we didn't try to escape, he wouldn't end our lives the way he'd ended Braydon and Pete's lives.

By the time the man stopped walking again and gave us water from the canteen he carried, I could feel Jake poking at the edge of my consciousness. I sat down next to Houston and closed my eyes.

"I'm here," I said in my mind. "We were hiking up the side of Lowman's Peak. It took all my concentration not to fall and slide right back down the face of the mountain."

"So, are you at the top of Lowman's Peak?" Jake asked in my head.

"We are. I don't think this guy is done hiking for the day, but that's where we are now. I'll contact you when we set out again."

I opened my eyes and turned to look at Houston when everything went black.

Chapter 12

"What happened?" I asked, although there was no one there to answer. I was in a cave with only a tiny sliver of light from an opening overhead. My arms were extended over my head. It seemed like they were tied to each other and then tied to a hook.

I closed my eyes as my head pounded. I wasn't sure what the madman had used, but he had hit me hard enough to knock me out and give me the mother of all headaches.

"Houston," I called out, hoping he was there even though I couldn't see him.

Either the sun was setting, or it had gone behind a cloud since the sliver of light that had been there before dimmed considerably. If the sun was going down, then that meant we could have traveled miles and miles before ending up here. How had I gotten here? I supposed either Houston or the kidnapper must have carried me.

I wanted to rub my head, but my arms were numb. I knew I was in a bad situation and wanted to panic, but I also knew panicking wouldn't do me any good. I took a deep breath and closed my eyes. I willed my mind to focus on Jake. I knew that he'd be looking for me and that his mind would be open and receptive enough to accept my presence in his head.

"Harmony? Is that you?"

I sighed in relief as I heard his voice in my head. "It's me."

"Oh, thank God. I've been trying to reach you all day. Where are you?"

"I'm not sure. I'm pretty sure I'm in a cave of some sort, but I don't know where. I've been unconscious since the last time we connected."

"Unconscious? What happened?"

I took a moment to fill him in. It had been seven hours since I'd connected with him the first time, which meant we could have traveled quite a long way. Of course, we could still be in the general vicinity of Lowman's Peak, and I might have been in this cave tied to the wall the entire time. I had no idea where I was or where Jake should start looking. Jake and the team had already headed toward the peak and hadn't found us, so they'd spread out a bit, but they'd been looking in the general area. They must be in the wrong area, or the dogs would have picked up my scent. I tried to describe what I could remember about the spot where we'd stopped to rest in greater detail. Once the dogs had my scent, I was sure they'd find us, no matter how far off the beaten path we might have ended up.

"Sitka has something," I heard Jake say in my head. "Hang on. We're coming for you."

I had no way of knowing how long it would take for the dogs to get to me since I had no way of knowing how far we'd traveled after I'd been knocked out. It made sense to me that the man hadn't traveled far carrying my unconscious body, so it was more likely than not that I was close by. As for Houston, I had no way of knowing what the madman had done with him. He might be stashed in the same cave as me. It was dark, so I couldn't see much beyond my immediate surroundings, and if he was unconscious, he wouldn't have responded when I'd called out to him. Or he might be conscious but stashed in a different cave. Even if he was in a different cave, he might still be in the area. And then, of course, there was the possibility that the kidnapper kept him walking, and he might be miles and miles away.

The sun had set by the time Jake and the team found me. I wanted to set out right away and look for Houston, and Jake wanted to wait for Dani so she could take me to the hospital to be checked out. Of course, there was nowhere for Dani to land without hiking away from the ridge, and there was no way I was going home without Houston, so we compromised and found a semi-flat place to set up the tents for a few hours. We'd have a quick meal and grab a few hours of sleep while we waited for the sun to rise. I had a feeling that tomorrow would be a very long day since there was no way I was leaving this wilderness without the entire team beside me.

Chapter 13

It appeared as if Houston had been with the kidnapper when I was brought to the cave. The team found a pair of gloves that belonged to Houston near where I was tied up. I supposed Houston had left them behind intentionally to give the dogs a scent to follow once they found me. I was grateful for Houston's quick thinking and faith that not only would the team find me but that they would pick up his trail too.

Once the sun came up, the trek went quickly. It was true that the kidnapper had a huge head start, and even if he'd stopped to sleep, as we had, we'd have to hurry to catch up. All three dogs had worked with Houston, and all seemed motivated to find him. I figured that if we kept going, we'd eventually catch up with him. I'd tried to connect with Houston on several occasions, but for some reason, he was one person I'd never been able to get through to. It was true that I wasn't able to connect with anyone at any time, and most of my connections had been with either injured individuals or serial killers, but there had been a few exceptions to this rule, Jake and Shredder, to name two, so I hoped that if I continued to try, Houston would let me in.

"The dogs have something," Jake said.

We all stopped walking as first Sitka, followed by Yukon and Kojak, took off running. The dogs had been off leash since we wanted to give them room to work, so once they took off, the entire team dropped their backpacks and took off after them.

When the dogs got to a cave opening much like the one I'd recently been rescued from, I called for them to wait. Thankfully, they did. Jake attached leashes to all three dogs and instructed Landon and me to hang onto them while he and Wyatt went inside. I wanted to go with Jake, but I was still a bit weak and shaky, and Jake pointed out that we had no idea what we'd find inside. After a bit of whining on my part, I finally agreed to wait outside the cave as Jake had wanted me to do in the first place.

"How long has it been?" I asked Landon.

"About ten minutes."

"That seems too long. We should go in."

"Jake said to wait, so we're going to wait." He looked down at the three dogs the two of us hung onto. "It might not be safe for the dogs to be inside.

We don't want to put them in danger if we don't need to."

"No," I agreed. "I don't want that, but it's taking so long. Why is it taking so long?"

Landon opened his mouth to respond when Jake and Wyatt emerged from the cave. There was a person between them who they seemed to be helping to walk, but it wasn't Houston.

"Logan?" I asked.

Jake nodded. "I'm sorry, Harm. We didn't find any evidence that Houston was anywhere in the area, but Logan was tied to a wall the same way you were."

I looked at the teen, who looked to be in decent health despite the trauma he'd likely endured. "Have you been in the cave all this time?"

He shook his head. "Grizz had me walking all over tarnation with him for days and days. It got worse after the others got away. He brought me to this cave yesterday. He tied me to a wall and told me he'd be back for me. I asked him where he was going, and he said he needed to check on something. When I heard footsteps, I assumed it was Grizz coming back for me." He glanced at the men on either side of him. "I'm really glad it was you all instead."

"We need to find a place for Dani to land, so she can pick Logan up and get him to a hospital," Jake said. He helped Logan over to a large flat rock and helped him to sit down. He offered him water and then looked at Wyatt. "Hike up to the top of that ridge and see if you can get a signal with your satellite phone. Once you have one, call Dani and fill her in, and then call Sarge and have him examine the topographical maps for the closest place for Dani to land."

I was really happy that we'd managed to find Logan alive, but waiting for Dani to come for him would delay our search for Houston. I knew Houston could take care of himself, but the kidnapper seemed to be the worst kind of crazy, and I worried that he'd become bored with dragging his newest victim around and would do away with him before we could find him.

"You were alone with the kidnapper for several days," I said to Logan.

He nodded. "After Carter was stabbed and the girls took off, I tried to run as well, but I tripped and fell on a rock. I think I cracked a rib. It definitely knocked the wind out of me. I tried to get up, but Grizz had caught up with me by the time I got my feet under my body."

"You keep referring to the kidnapper as Grizz. I thought his name was Steven Sullivan."

"He never mentioned his name, but he looked like a big grizzly bear of a man, so I started calling him Grizz."

I supposed that was as good a name as any.

"Did you find the others?" he asked.

"We did. The girls are all safe, and Carter is in the hospital, but it appears he'll pull through."

"Oh, thank goodness. I was terrified for Alice and Talia. They were my responsibility."

"Alice did become ill along the way, but I understand that she's on the road to recovery. As for Talia, she seemed to have fared well the entire time. I understand she's gone back to California."

"I'm glad to hear that. Once we'd all been taken by that madman, it occurred to me that it was my fault that both Alice and Talia were there, which made me responsible for them. Being responsible for two individuals in addition to myself was a lot more responsibility than I was prepared for and a lot more responsibility than I'm ever going to want to take on again."

"What you went through was traumatic. Once you have a chance to work through the trauma associated with the event, you may feel differently."

"Doubtful." He adjusted his position a bit. "I hate to ask, but do you know what happened to Braydon and Pete?"

"Neither teen made it. I'm really very sorry."

He bowed his head. "I figured as much. Braydon ran off after he was stabbed, but that was days and days ago. There was no way he'd survive on his own for that long. And Pete was bleeding so much after Grizz stabbed him that I knew he wasn't going to make it. Looking back, we never should have tried to confront the guy. I'm not sure what his long-term plan for us was, but he actually took care of us, and even though he made us aimlessly walk for days on end while he looked for Hope, he didn't hurt us until we attacked him."

"So he never mentioned why he took you or what he planned to do with you?" I asked.

Logan shook his head but then paused and shrugged. "Actually, there was one point when he said something about a 'trade.' He didn't talk much, and I don't think he ever said more than two words in a row the whole time I was with him, but I had a feeling that he was going to need someone to trade for Hope once he found her."

"Hope has been missing for a very long time. It's highly unlikely that he'll ever find her."

He raised a brow. "Really? He made it sound as if he'd only recently lost her."

"If the man who took you is Steven Sullivan, and if the Hope he's looking for is the daughter he lost, then the girl has been missing for twelve years."

"Twelve years?" He shook his head. "Based on the few things he said, I assumed the girl had been missing for weeks, not years. Poor guy. Don't get me wrong, I hate that this man killed two of my friends, but I was with him long enough to know he's truly grieving. If he has been living with such a huge burden for so many years, it's no wonder he's crazy." He rubbed his hands over his head. "I really don't know how I can thank you and the others for finding me. If this guy planned to hang onto me until he could trade me for Hope, it sounds as if he might never have set me free." He frowned. "I wonder why he left me in the cave."

"He came after my friend and me. He left me in a cave similar to the one he left you in, and my friends found me, but he still has Houston. Do you have any idea where he might have gone?"

Logan paused as if really considering the question. "As I said, he said something at one point about a trade. He didn't expand on the idea, so I don't know for certain that he was going to trade his captive for this Hope, but it makes sense that it was the reason he felt the need to take captives. He also mentioned something about a 'waking.' I'm not sure who or what would be waking, but it sounded like he had to wait for this 'waking' to occur. The guy has truly lost his mind. He barely speaks, and when he does, he babbles. Nothing he said made much sense, but I had a lot of time to put together the things he did say, and if I had to guess, the guy is waiting for someone or something to wake up so he can make a trade."

"Something?" I asked.

He shrugged. "I can't be sure, but I think he mentioned Anacartnia. The first night we camped, Pete told a campfire story about a big hairy man, similar to Bigfoot, who lived in the Alaskan wilderness. I'm pretty sure he called this monster Anacartnia. Pete was the brainy sort. He knew all sorts of things, including little-known facts that most people never heard of."

Jake walked over right about then to let us know that Dani was on her way. We'd need to hike two miles up to get over the mountain we were currently perched on, but it was the closest place Sarge could identify as being far enough away from the tall peaks in the area to make it safe for Dani to land. Of course, Jake wanted me to go with Logan and Dani, but there was no way I was going anywhere without Houston, so in the end, after delivering a new batch of supplies, Dani took Logan to the hospital, and Jake, Landon, Wyatt, the dogs, and I set off to find Houston and the madman who'd taken him.

Chapter 14

"Have you ever heard of Anacartnia?" I asked the men as we hiked.

"I have," Landon answered. "Anacartnia is the Alaskan equivalent of Sasquatch. Why do you ask?"

"When I was talking with Logan while we waited for Sarge to get back to us regarding a place for Dani to meet us, he mentioned that the man who'd kidnapped him had mentioned Anacartnia at one point. It seems Anacartnia is associated with a legend in the southwest region of Alaska and that the kidnapper believes a creature such as Anacartnia lives in this area as well."

"So, does this guy think Bigfoot has his daughter?" Wyatt asked.

"That seems to be what Logan believes after piecing together random statements made over time. Logan did admit the man tended to ramble when he spoke, which wasn't often, so he couldn't be certain of his intent." I paused. "Oh, and Logan also said that the man he called Grizz was waiting for him to wake up."

"Waiting for Anacartnia to wake up?" Wyatt clarified.

I nodded.

"I guess it makes sense that if there was a Bigfoot-type creature in the area, he'd likely hibernate," Landon said matter-of-factly.

I watched as Jake paused and looked out over the landscape.

"Do you see anything?" I asked him.

"No. The dogs seem to have lost the scent. I think we need to go back to the point where we felt they last had it. Rescuing Logan and then taking the detour to meet Dani has likely pulled us away from the route taken by Houston and the kidnapper. If we want to be certain we pick up Houston's scent, we should go back to the cave where we found Logan. The dogs were tracking Houston when we found Logan, which means that in addition to Logan being in the cave, Houston had been there at one point as well."

"Logan didn't mention that he'd seen Houston," I pointed out.

"True," Jake acknowledged. "But perhaps the kidnapper brought Houston to the cave but didn't take him inside. If Houston had never been to the cave where we found Logan, then the dogs wouldn't have ended up there."

Jake had a point since it was likely that Houston had been near the cave, if only for a few minutes. If he'd been anywhere in the vicinity, the dogs should be able to pick up his trail.

"It'll take hours to backtrack, but wandering aimlessly around the Alaskan wilderness isn't going to get us anywhere," Landon offered.

"Returning to the cave does seem to be the only choice we have at this point," Wyatt agreed.

I could see that poor Kojak was becoming more and more agitated the longer it took for us to find Houston. The dog was a rookie S&R dog, but he was highly motivated at this point. While I knew all the dogs would do their best to find Houston, I was willing to bet that Kojak would be the one who would find a way to bring his buddy home.

When we arrived at the cave where we'd found Logan, Jake gave all three dogs Houston's scent. The dogs all headed out in a southerly direction within a few minutes. Based on everything we knew about the man, it was reasonable to expect he would travel in a random pattern. I just hoped that if he'd crossed his own path along the way, it wouldn't confuse the dogs since there would be two scents to follow leading away from one central location.

I think we all hoped we'd find Houston today, but the kidnapper likely had a huge lead on us, which meant that it was going to be tough to catch up with him. It was getting cold and dark, so Jake instructed us to take a break and set up camp for the night.

"I hate sitting here when I know Houston is out there, and I have no idea whether or not he's okay," I said to the group as we ate our freeze-dried meal.

"I agree," Jake said. "But none of us will be able to help Houston if we get ourselves lost or hurt. It's cold and dark, and we're all exhausted. I think it's best that we try to get a few hours of shut-eye and then regroup."

I knew Jake was right, but that didn't cause me to like the situation any more than I had. I'd never be able to sleep as long as Houston was missing, but I promised Jake I would try and dutifully curled up with Yukon and closed my eyes. I must have slipped into slumber after all since the next thing I knew, I was dreaming.

"I've been waiting for you," a deep voice I realized was most likely the voice of the kidnapper said.

"Waiting for me? I've been trying to get in, but you've been keeping me out."

"I have," he admitted. "But I've been picking up on your attempts to reach the man you were traveling with. Interestingly, he doesn't seem receptive to your efforts, but after I began to pick up bits and pieces of your misguided transmissions, I realized that you might be a huge help to me."

"Help?" I asked. It had been a while since I'd connected to anyone in my dream state, but in this instance, I realized what was going on right away.

"My daughter, Hope, is missing. If you are able to psychically connect with people, then it occurred to me that you might be able to connect with her."

"Hope has been missing for twelve years," I pointed out.

"Really? Has it been that long? In some ways, it feels like I lost her just yesterday, and in other ways, it feels like I've been searching for her for a lifetime."

"Listen, I understand your desperation and need to find your daughter. I'm willing to do what I can, but I don't think you should expect too much. As I just indicated, it has been a very long time."

"Do you want to see your friend alive again?"

"Of course I do."

"Then you'll find her. If you find her, I'll let your friend go. If you don't…" he let the thought trail off.

I realized at that moment that as long as I was connected to the man, even if it was in my dream state, I had access to what he saw and heard. I doubted I could find Hope, mostly because I was pretty sure that she was likely dead, but by communicating with the man through my dreams, I would be able to find clues that might help me save Houston.

"I'd like to help you find your daughter, but I'm going to need more to go on than I have." I could see that the man was outside. It was dark, but there was a campfire. Houston was sitting about ten feet away from the fire. There were rocks in the background that he was leaning on. I could hear the sound of water rushing. I supposed the men might be near a waterfall or perhaps rapids.

"What do you need?" he asked.

"Tell me something about your daughter. What does she look like? What are some things she enjoyed doing before she was lost?"

"Taken."

"Taken?"

"Hope wasn't lost; she was taken."

Okay, that was new information. I didn't need any of the details I'd asked for in order to attempt a connection, but I wanted to keep the man talking so that I had more time to look around.

After a moment, the man began to speak. He not only spoke with his mind, but I sensed he spoke aloud as well. That was good. Maybe Houston would hear him speaking and realize I'd made a connection. Perhaps he could use that to communicate with me.

"What does Hope look like? Hair color and that sort of thing."

"Blond hair, blue eyes, and a smile like an angel."

I watched Houston while the man spoke. I tried to decide if he was moving. I didn't notice movement, so perhaps he was sleeping. I knew I needed more time to figure out where the men were camping, so I decided to keep the man talking.

"Can you picture her in your mind?"

An image of a young girl with a huge grin came to mind. I could feel this man's love for the child. Real love. Deep and caring. The type of deep emotion that could strip you of your sanity and humanity if it was taken away from you.

"Someone is calling to me," I said. "Once I wake up, I'll likely lose the connection. Please tell me where to find you. I'll come to you, and together, we'll look for Hope."

He hesitated.

"Please. I want to help you, but I'm not sure I will be able to reconnect once I wake up."

"Come alone."

"I will," I promised.

"If you lie to me or bring the others with you, your friend will die."

"Understood."

The man looked at Houston. "You love him."

"I do," I admitted.

"Then don't gamble with his life. I know you are thinking that you will promise one thing and do another, but you should know that I can read your mind during those times we are connected as you are reading mine."

With that, I awoke. Before the connection was lost, however, the kidnapper revealed to me the location of his campsite. Of course, now I had a significant decision to make. Did I find a way to ditch Jake and the others and go to Houston on my own as I'd promised, or did I assume that the man was lying about being able to read my mind and take a chance and bring reinforcements?

Chapter 15

After a lot of thought, I decided I couldn't risk Houston's life by telling anyone where I was going. If Jake knew what I was planning, he'd never allow me to head out on my own, so the only option open to me seemed to be to find a way to sneak away. I didn't want Jake to worry when he realized I was missing, so I knew I'd also need to find a way to tell him what I was doing but not where I was going. The timing and execution of the whole thing were going to be dicey, but I owed it to Houston to do everything within my power to save his life.

I only had an hour of darkness left before the sun began to lighten the sky. If I took only the time of day into account, it made sense to sneak away now. But I was trapped in a tent with Jake and all three dogs, so there was no way I was going anywhere without everyone knowing what I was doing. No, I thought to myself, I'd have to find a way to sneak away after we'd hit the trail for the day. Part of me wanted to tell Jake what I'd seen and what I knew, but then I remembered the kidnapper's warning.

In the end, I decided not to tell Jake that I'd connected with the kidnapper during my sleep. At least not yet. I knew that the kidnapper had taken Houston to the lake that everyone called Little Sister. Little Sister was the first of three lakes that were linked by a wilderness trail called Three Sisters. The Three Sisters Lakes weren't an area we'd covered during our rescue mission so far, but I had a feeling that once Jake began to put things together, he'd figure out exactly what was going on and follow me anyway. The reality was that once I slipped away, the dogs would pick up my trail without my having to break my promise to the crazy kidnapper, who may or may not be able to read my mind.

"It seems as if the dogs wanted to head toward Little Sister Lake at that last intersection," Wyatt said. "I know the plan was to head to Sapphire Lake, but I think that we should consider changing course."

"I feel like I have an image in my head of Sapphire Lake," I lied.

"Maybe you should check again," Landon said. "I know you haven't had any luck connecting with Houston, but I'd hate to hike all the way out to Sapphire Lake only to find out that the guy headed up to Three Sisters."

"I'll try again," I said. "I'll need a quiet place to work. Maybe you can give the dogs fresh water and something to eat. I worry that Yukon, in particular, isn't getting enough calories."

"Okay. I'll take care of the dogs," Landon said.

Jake had wandered off to call Dani. She was waiting for instructions before heading out from Rescue. I wasn't sure what he was saying to her, but it seemed like the pair had been talking for a long time.

With both Landon and Jake busy, I just needed to ditch Wyatt. He was sitting on a log, eating a granola bar. He didn't seem to be paying any attention to me, so I slowly backed into the forest and hoped he wouldn't notice that I'd disappeared until I could get far enough away from the men for them not to follow or inquire about my movements.

If I was going to head up to Three Sisters, I needed to hurry. Once the guys realized I was missing, I knew they'd use the dogs to track me. It wasn't that I didn't want them to find me because I did, eventually. I just didn't want them to find me too soon. The kidnapper had told me I had to come alone or Houston would die. At this point, I had to assume that if I told the others where I was heading, the man would know and follow through with his threat. That meant that if my friends were going to save us, they were going to have to figure the whole thing out on their own.

To be honest, I was surprised I'd been able to sneak away. Everyone was exhausted and not nearly as alert as they usually were, and Jake and Landon were both distracted when I slipped away. Depending on the length of Jake's call, I supposed I might have a ten or fifteen-minute head start. I knew I needed to hurry, so I dug deep to access whatever energy I had left and moved toward my destination as quickly as I could. When I arrived at Little Sister Lake, I found the man, who I believed to be the kidnapper, sitting on a rock looking out over the lake. Houston was nowhere in sight.

"Where's Houston?" I asked.

"He's safe. Once you return Hope to me, I'll return your friend to you."

I slowly approached. I didn't sense that the man wanted to harm me, so I accepted his offer when he offered me a seat on a nearby log.

"I want to start by saying that while I am willing to do what I can to help you find Hope, I'm not always able to connect. You observed that yourself when I began trying to connect with Houston once I woke up alone in the cave. As you are aware, I've been unsuccessful in my effort. Establishing a connection is a two-way street. The person I'm connecting with has to be receptive to my presence."

"I understand. Hope is a child. She has the willingness to believe in things she doesn't understand. She'll let you in."

"If Hope is still alive, she's twenty-six."

The man frowned. I think his mind was damaged to the extent that he simply could not accept the reality of the passage of time. I supposed it was in my best interests at this point to allow him to believe that I would be able to connect with Hope. Doing so would give me time to figure out a way to make him tell me where he'd stashed Houston. It was true that since I knew that Houston had been here at the lake a few hours earlier, it was reasonable to expect that the dogs could pick up his scent and find him even without the help of the kidnapper, but I didn't want to take that risk if I didn't have to.

"I didn't tell the others where I was going as per our agreement, but my friends will come looking for me once they realize I'm gone. We should get started."

He nodded.

"I want you to think of Hope. I want you to envision the last time you saw her. I am going to try to piggyback on your memory. I'm hoping that if I can grab onto your emotion and connection to your daughter, it will help me to connect as well."

The man looked uncertain. He didn't say he wouldn't do as I asked, but he didn't make a move to carry out my request either. I knew that what I was asking was a lot, and I knew that there was virtually no way I was going to connect with this child who likely died twelve years ago even if he did cooperate, but I knew that the only way to save Houston was to try, so I planned to do just that.

"What do you want me to do?" he asked.

"I want you to close your eyes and relax. I'm going to talk you through it. Don't try to think. Just feel. I'm going to try to observe your memories, but just ignore me. Don't try to control the situation. Just relax and allow your mind to follow my voice."

His brow puckered.

"It really is the only way. It's been so long."

He grunted, sat in front of the log I was sitting on, and leaned against it. He gave me a single look of suspicion and then closed his eyes. It was my hope that once I got in, if I was even able to do so, I'd have access to all of his memories, including the memory of the location where he'd stashed Houston.

"Okay, we're going to begin by remembering back to the camping trip you took with Hope. The last trip you took together before she went missing."

"Was taken."

"Okay. Was taken. I'm looking for the memory of a happy moment. A moment that occurred on the timeline before when Hope was taken, but on the same trip."

An image of a healthy, clean-cut man with thick sandy hair fishing on the bank of a lake I was pretty sure might be Middle Sister Lake appeared in his mind. There was a blond-haired girl standing next to him. The two weren't speaking or communicating in any way, but they gave the impression that they were content sharing a quiet moment. The day was sunny and bright, but I could sense that it was late in the day based on the shadows portrayed on the sheer granite cliffs that surrounded this particular lake. It occurred to me that Middle Sister Lake would be a good place for the kidnapper to have stashed Houston since it was close to our current location and featured many shallow caves created by the rocky walls of the gorge where the lake was located.

"It's late in the day, it's warm and sunny, and you are fishing with Hope," I said in a soft voice. "The scene appears serene, but I sense an underlying tension."

"Hope didn't want to come camping with me that weekend. She had a party to attend, but we'd planned the trip for months, so I made her go."

I could feel the connection slipping as what I initially thought was a happy memory turned toward something dark.

"Hope had been canceling on you a lot," I said. "The little girl who'd helped you fight your way back from some sort of trauma was growing up and had her own friends and a life outside of the life she shared with you."

"It was that boy. Everything was fine until that boy came along and ruined everything."

I knew that I'd need to understand the entire story if I was going to help this man, but I didn't want to get too far off track and lose the connection since what I was really after was a hint as to where Houston was stashed.

"Hope was angry with you for making her come along on the trip with you."

I could tell by his response and rise in heart rate that this was indeed a fact.

"She didn't want to go fishing that day, but you made her."

Again, I felt sure that I was on the right track.

"She fished silently next to you, refusing to share in the fun and laughter as she had in the past."

I felt the man's anger turn to pain.

"Hope was hurting that day. She'd made plans with friends, which you ruined with your trip. She fished quietly for a while, and then she lashed out."

The pain the man was feeling melted into rage. "It was just the two of us after I got home from the war and her mother left. I'd been in such a dark place, but Hope was my salvation." He took a deep breath. "I thought I was hers. I couldn't believe the hurtful things she said before she ran." The man opened his eyes, and the connection was broken. "That's enough of that. I know what happened on the day she ran off. What I don't know is where she is now."

"You said that someone took Hope."

He nodded. "Anacartnia."

"Did you see this large hairy man take your daughter?"

Again, he nodded. "After Hope ran, I went after her. I wasn't watching where I was going, and when I came around a corner, I found myself face-to-face with the hairy man. I ran, and he ran after me. I was sure I was dead, but Hope screamed, and when I turned around, I saw that he had changed course and had taken Hope."

I put my hand to my mouth to stifle a groan. The hairy man who took Hope rather than her father was likely a grizzly bear, but I didn't say as much at this point.

"If this man took Hope, why do you think she's still alive?"

"I did some research. The hairy man who lives in this part of Alaska prefers nuts and berries to meat. It's likely that the man who took Hope took her for companionship and not as a meal. According to lore, if I offer a trade, he will return that which was taken from me."

"And that's why you kidnapped the teens."

Again, he didn't answer. It was obvious that the man had completely lost his mind at some point. I suspected that there had been a time when the man knew that the hairy man who'd taken his daughter while sparing his life had been a bear and not a Bigfoot-type creature, but accepting the reality of a bear attack was simply too much for his mind to handle, so he'd created the story about Anacartnia. A mythical creature taking Hope meant there was still a chance of getting her back. I think it was this fantasy that he'd clung to all of these years. The question was, how did I use this knowledge to find Houston?

"The hairy man took Hope from a location near here," I said.

An image of a rocky ledge near Middle Sister Lake flashed through his mind.

"It's important that I know what exactly happened if I am going to find her," I said as the memory faded, and I could feel the connection slip away. I guessed I didn't blame the man for not wanting to dig at that particular memory, but he eventually closed his eyes, and I could feel him slipping into the quiet space at the back of his mind where memories are stored. The sound of dogs barking in the distance told me that Jake and the others had found me. I'd hoped for more time, but once the man I was with heard the dogs, he jumped up and grabbed his gun.

"Hope is dead," I said as the man pointed his gun at me.

He lowered his gun. "I know. I wouldn't allow myself to believe it before, but you cleared things out a bit when you were digging around in my memories. A bear, not a Bigfoot-type creature, took Hope. The large bear came at me until Hope screamed, then turned and went for her." He began to sob. "She should have stayed quiet. She should have hidden in a small space the way I showed her to do. It didn't have to happen that way." He raised his gun and put it to his temple.

"No," I yelled as his finger slowly pulled the trigger, ending this man's pain once and for all.

I ran to his side to check for a pulse, but it was obvious he was dead.

Jake and the dogs came running over the summit of the small mountain leading up to the lower lake. The panicked look on his face was enough to tell me that when he'd heard the shot, he believed it was me who'd lost my life. Yukon jumped up to greet me, and Jake pulled me into his arms. "Oh my God, Harm." He hugged me hard enough to squeeze the breath from my lungs. "When I heard the shot…"

"I know." I tried to put a bit of distance between us so that I could breathe freely. "I'm fine."

He took a step back, placing his hands on my shoulders. "Are you crazy? Why on earth would you come and pay a visit to a man who we know killed two teenagers and injured another?"

"He has Houston. It was the only way." A tear rolled down my cheek. "He promised to tell me where he'd stashed Houston if I agreed to help him. He died before he did."

Jake hugged me again as Wyatt and Landon joined us. "Don't worry. We'll find him."

"I think he might be at Middle Sister Lake. I'm not certain, but I know he was here last night, so the man who kidnapped him must have stashed him somewhere nearby."

"Landon will wait here with the body, and Wyatt and I will go with you to take a look." Jake turned toward Landon. "Once we climb out of this valley on our way to access Middle Sister, there should be reception for the satellite phones. I'll call Dani and have her head in this direction. The cliffs are steep, but the area near the lake is pretty open. Dani should be able to land on the meadow side of Little Sister without too much of a problem."

"I'll keep an eye out for her," Landon promised.

"We'll come back here after checking out Middle Sister whether we find Houston or not. If he's not there, we'll work together to come up with an alternate plan." Jake still had Houston's gloves, so he gave the dogs the scent, and we followed as they headed up out of the gorge toward Middle Sister as I'd suspected they would.

The hike up to Middle Sister Lake from Little Sister Lake usually took a couple hours, but today we were motivated and made it in less than an hour. There were a lot of places to hide a person, especially a person who was either unconscious or gagged and couldn't call out, so we hoped the dogs would be able to find the exact location where the kidnapper had stashed Houston, if he was indeed up here.

"The kidnapper might have taken Houston to Big Sister," Jake said after we'd been looking for an hour with no luck. "It's only about an hour from here."

I looked at the dogs who were staring at the cliff face behind the lake as if expecting to see Houston magically appear.

"The dogs followed the trail to the granite cliff at the rear of the lake. I have no idea how the kidnapper would have gotten Houston up there, but I suspect he's up there all the same." I placed the binoculars I'd been using against my eyes. "There's a slight opening about three-quarters of the way up. It's narrow but tall. From here, it looks like a fit adult could squeeze through."

"How did he get Houston up there?" Wyatt asked.

"Maybe Houston voluntarily climbed up. He likely would have if the kidnapper had a gun on him and told him to climb."

Jake frowned as he studied the face of the cliff. "I suppose an experienced climber could make it up to the opening you're referring to. I have a rope in my backpack. I suppose I can give it a try."

"I'll go," I said.

"I'll go," Wyatt overrode my intention. "I have the most rock-climbing experience by far."

"We all have experience," I countered.

"Wyatt will go," Jake said. "We all have experience, but Wyatt does have the most."

The granite face beyond the lake didn't provide many footholds, but Wyatt eventually made it to the small opening I'd noticed. He slipped inside and then slipped out less than a minute later.

"The space beyond the opening is small. There's no one there, and there isn't any evidence that anyone ever was here. I know all the dogs came to a halt at the granite ridge, which makes it seem as if Houston climbed up, but I suspect that he simply climbed up to that first ledge and then made his way around to the back of the granite wall where the trail leading to Big Sister can be accessed."

"I'm heading up," I said. "The dogs won't make it up without harnesses, so someone will need to stay with them."

"I'll go to Big Sister with Harmony," Jake said to Wyatt. "You head back to Little Sister and check in with Landon. Dani should be on her way. She should be able to land at both Big Sister and Little Sister, and radio access should be clear now that we're out of the gorge. If we get into trouble, we'll call her."

I could hear Yukon howling as Jake and I left him behind, but he couldn't come, and I needed to go, so he would have to be unhappy for a couple hours until I could return. He had Wyatt, Landon, and the other dogs, so I knew he'd be fine. We'd spent a fair amount of time apart on this particular trip, so I wasn't sure why he was having a fit now when he'd seemed okay with these little separations along the way. If I didn't know better, I'd say he could sense danger of some sort. Of course, it was more likely that he was simply tired of being left behind and wanted to come with me on whatever adventure I was heading out on.

"Do you hear something?" I asked Jake as I placed my hand on my rifle, turned the corner, and came face to face with one of the largest bears I'd ever seen.

Chapter 16

"Don't move," Jake instructed.

I knew not to move, but I wasn't going to reply since not moving meant not moving *anything*, including my mouth. The bear was large but not as large as I'd first thought. She didn't have cubs, at least not that I could see, which was good since mama bears tended to be twitchy. She'd been eating from a berry bush when I'd turned the corner, and after looking me up and down a bit and likely deciding I was too scrawny to provide much of a danger, she returned to her snack. Jake trained his rifle on the gorgeous animal as I very, very slowly backed away. I knew it was never a good idea to make major or quick movements, and there was no way I, or anyone, could outrun a bear, so my best bet was simply to take my time and slowly disappear from her line of vision.

"She has tags," Jake said after the bear turned her head to look closer. Bears who'd been captured in the past for one reason or another received different color tags in their ears, so they could be identified. While many tagged bears only spent a short time in captivity, some no longer than it took to examine and tag them, others had been injured, cared for, and released. Those bears had experienced human contact, hopefully in a good way, and could be less likely to act aggressively at times. Of course, bears, even those who'd temporarily been housed in a domestic situation, were still wild animals and, therefore, unpredictable.

Once I'd backed around the corner, Jake motioned for me to join him at the forest's edge. Unfortunately, our bear was currently dining not ten feet from the trail we'd need to travel to access Big Sister Lake, which meant we were in a holding pattern until she moved.

"Have you tried connecting with Houston?" Jake asked once we'd carefully moved a safe distance away from the bear, who appeared to be taking her sweet time.

"I have. I've never been able to connect with Houston. Even when I was looking for Shredder and Houston this past June, it was Shredder who I was able to connect with. I'm not sure if Houston is intentionally blocking me, which I guess I can somewhat understand if he is, or if we just don't have the right chemistry to make a two-way connection."

"Chemistry?" he asked.

I shrugged. "It's not like I can connect with anyone I want to connect with. I've connected with you in the past when there was a need for you to rescue me, and I seem to be able to connect with Shredder without any problem. I'm not sure how it works exactly, but short of intense emotion to use as a catalyst, such as pain or extreme fear, I think there needs to be a level of openness and trust."

"So are you saying that you trust me and you trust Shredder, but you don't trust Houston?"

I frowned. "I don't think it's that. I love Houston. I may even be in love with him. And if I think about putting my life in his hands, I realize I also trust him. I think the problem with us making a connection has more to do with him not trusting me."

Jake raised a brow.

"Have I ever hurt you?" I asked.

"No. Of course not. Pissed me off a few times, sure, but never hurt."

"Does my presence in any way make you feel that you might be in some sort of danger simply due to my presence?" I added.

"No. The opposite, in fact. I always feel better about things when you are around."

"As much as I wish it was different, Houston can't honestly say that he hasn't been hurt by me. At least not physically. If not for me, Houston would never have been in the life-and-death situation he found himself in this past June."

"The man is a cop," Jake pointed out. "He expects a certain amount of danger in his life."

"Maybe. But I feel like something changed after the kidnapping. I hope we can get back to where we were before that whole thing went down, but I'm just not sure that's possible." I glanced toward the grove of berries where the bear had been eating. "It looks like we have a clear path. Let's get going before she comes back."

The remainder of the hike up to Big Sister was uneventful. When we arrived, we found shallow caves with narrow openings, much as we'd found at the two lakes lower in elevation. I didn't see Houston, and he hadn't called out to us when we'd called out to him, but I could sense a presence.

"I'll check that little cave over on the ridge, and you check for openings on the back side of the lake," I suggested to Jake.

"Stay alert. I don't sense any people or animals in the area, but I guess you never know."

Squeezing into the narrow opening of the cave I'd been headed toward hadn't been easy, which made me wonder how the kidnapper had gotten Houston inside.

"Are you okay?" I asked as I knelt down beside him to rip the tape from his mouth.

"I'm okay," he said after gasping for air. "The tape partially covered my nose in addition to my mouth, so I feel seriously oxygen deprived, but I'll be okay." He looked around. "Are you here alone?"

I got to work untying the ropes from his wrists and ankles. "Jake is here. I'll get you free, and then I'll let him know that I found you."

"The kidnapper?"

"Dead."

Houston flinched.

"By his own hand, not mine. He told me about the bear just before he died."

"Bear?" Houston asked.

"It's kind of a long story. I'll catch you up after we get out of here."

Houston attempted to stand and then flinched.

"What is it?" I asked.

"I think I broke my ankle. It'll be fine, but I'm going to have to take it slow."

"Dani is coming with the bird. She can give you a ride down the mountain."

Chapter 17

It had been two weeks since the team finally made it back to Rescue. Three people were dead, and six other lives had been irrevocably changed. It was hard for me to understand how the mind of a man who'd once been a soldier and a loving father could decay to the point where he'd commit murder and suicide. I knew that he'd been seriously grieving for a very long time. His wife had left, and his daughter was dead, and it was likely he didn't have much of a support system. I hated to think that a mind could simply slip into an illusion the way his mind had, but after everything he'd shared, I supposed it might have been the guilt more than the grief that had gotten to him.

"So Hope's mother left her father and took Hope with her," I said after having engaged in a long conversation with Sarge, who had continued his research even after those of us who could walk away had walked away. For some reason, Sarge was interested in getting the rest of the story and had even talked to Hope's friends and neighbors.

"As far as I can tell, that's exactly what occurred," Sarge said. "Hope's father had mental health problems after he returned from overseas, which his wife had used to argue that he was unfit to be a guardian. Even a part-time guardian. In the end, the court gave the mother full custody. Her only concession to her ex-husband was to allow him to take Hope camping once or twice a year. The trips were important to Hope's father, and initially, they were important to Hope as well, but then she got older and preferred to hang out with friends rather than her father, creating a conflict not just between Hope and her father but between Hope's parents as well."

"So it's likely that the ill-fated camping trip was doomed before it began," I said.

"In a way," Sarge agreed. "I don't claim to know all the specifics, but I do know that Hope and her father had argued about whether or not she should continue to be required to go on these weekend trips. Hope's mother sided with her, and at one point, Hope was told that it would be okay to go to the party with her friends, but then her dad showed up, and there was a huge blowout between Hope's mother and father, so in the end, Hope went with her dad simply to keep the peace."

I felt so bad for everyone involved. I was sure the trip had been fraught with fighting and hurt feelings right up to the point where Hope had run off.

"I still don't quite understand why Hope's father made up the Bigfoot story," Wyatt said.

"I'm not sure he made it up exactly," I said. "In the beginning, he must have known that the bear who'd been heading for him had ended up killing Hope, and the guilt must have eaten at him. I'm sure he had the need to fix things, but Hope being drug away by a huge grizzly bear isn't the sort of thing that can be fixed."

Sarge jumped in. "I can't say that I have all the details, but based on what those I've spoken to have said, things began to change at some point in the man's mind and memory. He actually seemed to think that this mythological creature had taken Hope, and if he could find her, he could trade for her return. He spent the next twelve years looking for her."

The whole thing sounded crazy, but I supposed that I understood the need of one's mind to make sense of something that hurt too deeply to accept and make peace with yet couldn't be reversed. I wondered about the years that no one had heard from the crazy hiker looking for his lost daughter, and Sarge shared that the man had spent a few years in jail for assault. As Sarge had stated when he began the conversation, the man wasn't mentally stable. I supposed there was no way to know how his life might have turned out had he not lost Hope and started down the rabbit hole in his attempt to find her and replace her in his life, but I suspected that he would have had a rough go of things in any circumstance.

"Houston called to make sure I was having my rib special tonight," Sarge said. "Are the two of you grabbing a meal?"

"No. I haven't heard from Houston all week. I went by Monday to make sure he was doing okay with his broken ankle, and he said he was and that a friend was going to come and stay with him until he could get around better."

"Maybe he's bringing the friend to Neverland as a thank you," Wyatt said.

"Maybe." I glanced at the clock on the wall. "I guess I should get going. I still have dogs to walk, cat boxes to clean, and a barn to shuck out."

"Are you off tonight?" Wyatt asked.

I nodded. "I thought I'd hang out with Chloe. It's been forever since the two of us got together. We talked about going over to Serena's to meet her new puppy. At least Chloe still needs to meet her. I met the pup at the shelter before Serena even took her home."

"She brought the pup by yesterday," Sarge said. "Sure is a cute little thing. All the pups from the litter are pretty darn cute. If I didn't already have Gunther, I'd have a look at the pups myself."

I had to smile at that. Sarge had never wanted a dog until I'd asked him to foster Gunther, and now the pair was the best of friends."

"I'm surprised you haven't scooped one up for yourself," Sarge added.

"Puppies are fun, but, as you know, I have more than my share of pets already and certainly don't need another one."

"I guess you have a point. If your plans with Chloe fall through, come on by. Even if you aren't working, I'll set some ribs back for you."

"I'd appreciate that. I'll take them home tomorrow if I don't make it in tonight. It's been a while since you made ribs."

"They wouldn't be special if I made them too often, now would they?"

I guessed Sarge had a point. Ribs weren't on the regular menu and were only offered occasionally as a special. Once word got out that Sarge's ribs could be had, nearly the whole town showed up for a few.

After I left Neverland, I headed home to walk the dogs. It was a gorgeous summer day with hours of sunlight left, making it seem reasonable to relax a bit and while away an afternoon. There had been a lot of bear activity in the area, so I grabbed my rifle as I always did when I left the cabin for any reason. I slowly walked at the back of the pack with Honey, Lucky, Juno, and Kodi while Denali, Yukon, and Shia took up positions in the front. I wasn't too worried about the three large dogs at the front of the pack in terms of encounters with wildlife; it was the older, weaker dogs who walked in the rear with me that I most needed to keep an eye on.

The lake behind my property had warmed a bit, so I slipped my shoes off and waded while the dogs, who liked to swim, took a dip. Lucky wasn't a fan of the water, so he found a spot under a shady tree. Kodi and Juno would splash around for a moment or two, but they seemed to prefer a nap to additional activity.

"Hey, Harley," I said after answering my cell phone, which had been buzzing in my pocket, although I hadn't noticed at first since the ringer was off. "What's up?"

"Sarge's ribs. I thought I'd head over to Neverland around six-thirty and grab a plate. Do you want to come with me?"

"I do, but I'm supposed to meet up with Chloe and Serena later. Maybe we can all go."

"Sounds fine with me. Do you just want to meet there?"

"Let's. I'm not sure what Chloe has in mind, but if we arrange to meet at six-thirty, that should work out fine. I'll call Sarge and have him reserve a table for us. The place is always crowded on ribs night."

"Okay. I'll see you there," Harley said before disconnecting the call. A quick call to Chloe confirmed that she was okay with allowing Harley to buy her a meal. Harley hadn't necessarily said he was paying, but when you went out with Harley Medford, he always paid.

After I hung up with Chloe, I called Serena and filled her in on the plan.

"Harley called and invited you to dinner?" she asked. Her words seemed neutral, but her tone was anything but.

"He invited us to dinner for ribs night. I reserved a table for four. Harley's going to meet us there, but I know Chloe wanted to stop by your place to see the new puppy. Maybe we can come by, and then the three of us can drive to Neverland together. Parking is always an issue on rib night."

"I guess that would be fine. What time will you be by?"

"Maybe five? We're meeting Harley at six-thirty. Chloe closes the café at two and is usually home by three-thirty, so we'd planned to hang out after that."

"I'll be at the shelter until five-thirty. Maybe I should just meet you at Neverland. Chloe can come by and see the puppy after we eat."

"Okay. Sounds good. I'll see you at six-thirty."

I couldn't help but frown after I hung up. I knew that Serena had a thing for Harley. She'd been panting after him almost as long as she'd worked at the shelter. And I supposed if I really stopped and thought about it, it might seem odd to Serena that Harley had called and asked me to dinner rather than her. But Harley and I were friends. Good friends. We frequently shared a meal as one friend with another. Serena knew that. I wasn't sure why she'd be jealous of my relationship with Harley if, indeed, she was jealous. Maybe I'd misread things. I did that sometimes. Ask any of my friends, and they'd be quick to tell you that while I am a whiz at search and rescue, I'm hopeless when it comes to relationships and the verbal and physical cues that come along with them.

Chloe and I arrived at Neverland a few minutes before either Harley or Serena, which provided me time to say hi to Houston and his friend. His exceedingly attractive female friend. Perhaps I was beginning to understand why Serena might be bent out of shape after all.

"It's so good to see you." I bent over and kissed him on the cheek. "How's your ankle?"

"It's much better, thanks to Hallery's help."

Hallery? I turned and smiled at the woman sitting across from Houston. "It's nice to meet you. How exactly do the two of you know each other?"

"Houston and I grew up living across the street from one another. Initially, he was friends with my brother, but then we realized that we had more in common with each other than he had with my brother, so the two of us began hanging out. I understand that you were part of the team that saved my Houston from that very bad madman on the mountain. I want you to know how grateful I am that you protected him in such a dangerous situation."

I tried not to cringe when she said, "my Houston," and I tried not to care that she made Houston sound weak. Instead, I offered her my most sincere smile, and with a tone that bordered on aggressive, I said, "Houston is part of Rescue, Alaska's search and rescue team. He's a very capable outdoorsman who has rescued his share of individuals during these operations. It is true that he was the one who was injured and in need of assistance this time, but I guess that's part of being a rescue worker here in Alaska, where every minute in the wilderness presents an elevated level of danger. I can assure you that at no point did Houston need protecting."

I shot Houston a look of apology for getting so huffy with his friend, and then I glanced over my shoulder at the table Sarge had reserved. "I really should get going. My friends are waiting. It was really good to meet you."

"And it was nice to meet you as well, dear."

Dear? Did that bleached blond bimbo just call me dear?

I swear Houston quirked his mouth to the left just a bit as I walked away. Did the man find his fluffy blond beach babe and her condescending comments funny?

Chapter 18

Despite the rocky start to the evening, Harley and I had an enjoyable night. Five minutes after we arrived, Chloe ran into her crush of the moment and left with him. A few minutes after Chloe left, Serena called and informed me that she had a headache and was just going to stay in. She'd seemed fine when I'd spoken to her earlier, but after seeing Houston with Hallery, I guessed I sort of understood how she might feel about me being such good friends with Harley.

"We're friends, right?" I asked Harley after he walked me out to my car following our shared meal.

"We are."

"And friends sometimes ask each other awkward questions about sensitive subjects, don't they?"

He hesitated. "Where are you going with this?"

I took a deep breath and brought up the subject that was on my mind. "I guess I'm just curious about your relationship with Serena. Not that it's any of my business, but sometimes I feel like I'm getting in the middle of things between the two of you."

Harley ran his hand through his long thick hair. I couldn't help but feel a catch in my throat as his hair fell into place over his ears. It didn't seem all that long ago that I'd spent hours doodling Mrs. Harley Medford on my bookbinder. At the time, I still wondered what would have happened if his dad hadn't died and his mom hadn't decided to move the family to LA.

"I'm aware that Serena has feelings for me and that she hopes for more than just the friendship I have to offer. Serena is kind and generous, and while I consider her to be one of my best friends, I'm afraid I'm just not looking for the sort of relationship I suspect she would like us to have. I guess I've been using you as a buffer of sorts. I would never want to hurt Serena, and I know that even taking a tiny step toward something more between us would only lead to heartache, so I guess I've gone out of my way to keep things between us professional. I'm sorry if I've put you in the middle."

I placed a hand on his. "It's okay. I get it. I really do. Serena is looking for a fairytale ending, and you've said on many occasions that you aren't ready for that. I can't even imagine trying to maintain a relationship of the romantic sort when you travel as much as you do. And while Serena has said that she'd follow you anywhere, I know she's actually a homebody at heart." I cringed. "Forget I said that last thing. I probably spoke out of turn."

"It's fine. I know how Serena feels. Trying to maintain the friendship as well as the business relationship while not introducing anything else into the mix seems to be getting harder and harder."

"Maybe you should just tell her how you feel. I know that it will be both difficult and awkward to do so, and she might give you the cold shoulder for a while, but Serena isn't dumb. She'll eventually realize how much she cares about both your friendship and the working relationship you share, and she'll find a way to manage her expectations."

He smiled. "You make it all sound so easy, but trust me when I say that managing expectations when it comes to the strong emotions associated with love isn't always as easy as it seems it should be."

Boy, didn't I know that to be true.

He leaned forward and offered me a friendly kiss on the lips. "I need to get home to Brando. He's entered a new chewing phase, which he uses to punish me if I leave him for too long. How about I call you tomorrow, and we can try to work through the situation between Serena and me and how I might manage it so as not to lose a valuable friendship."

"Are you saying that Hollywood heartthrob, Harley Medford, wants dating advice from little ol' me?"

"If by dating advice, you mean dating avoidance advice, then yes. You and Serena are friends. I value your input. If there is any way to do this without hurting her, then I need to take my time and figure this out."

I opened the door to my Jeep and climbed in. "Okay. Call me tomorrow. But not too early. I have a very firm plan to sleep in."

The drive home on a clear night was not a long one. When I pulled into my drive, I noticed Houston's truck sitting in front of my doorway. I pulled my Jeep into my favorite parking spot and slipped out. "Is everything okay?" I asked, figuring that everything must not be okay for him to show up unannounced like this.

"Everything is fine," he said. "I just thought we should talk."

Uh oh. "Okay. Come on in. Coffee?" I asked as I opened the door and greeted my menagerie.

"No. I think I've had enough coffee for one night." He crossed and then uncrossed his arms as if he was nervous or scared.

"Are you sure that everything is okay?"

He crossed his arms again, took a half step forward, and then paused. "I just wanted to let you know that Hallery and I really are just friends. And not even close friends as she made it seem. Really, we're just casual friends who used to know each other a very long time ago. She came to Alaska for a research project and called me, looking for lodging recommendations. As you know, if you don't have a reservation at this time of the year well in advance, you aren't going to get one, and she was only going to be here a week, so I invited her to stay in my spare room."

I wasn't sure why he was telling me all of this, but I offered him a half smile. "That was nice of you, and it is true that you can't just walk into any lodging property and get a room at this time of the year."

He cleared his throat and tried again. "Things have been a little weird between us since our ordeal with Shredder."

Okay, now things were getting serious. "Yes," I agreed. "I have felt that things have been off between us. I guess that can be expected. What happened to both of us was intense."

"It was. And I needed time to think things through and get my head on straight."

My heart rate accelerated just a bit. "And is it? On straight."

He paused without answering. I guessed I was hoping for something a bit more definitive at this point.

"Houston?" I asked when he still didn't speak after quite a few seconds.

He looked in my direction.

"Your head? Is it on straight?"

He smiled. "Honestly, I'm not sure. But I've been giving the situation a lot of thought, and I think I finally know what I want."

Please, please, please don't say that you are going to go back to Boston. "And what is it that you want?"

He closed the space between us, cupped my cheeks in his hands, and tilted my head until our eyes met, and then, ever so agonizingly slowly, he lowered his lips to mine.

Look for Finding Destiny in 2024

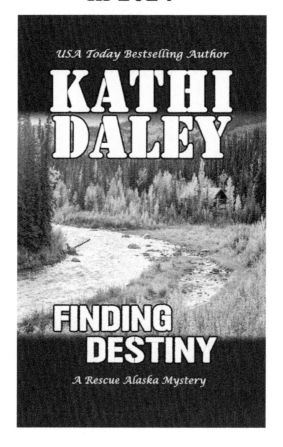

USA Today best-selling author Kathi Daley lives in beautiful Lake Tahoe with her husband, Ken. When she isn't writing, she likes spending time hiking the miles of desolate trails surrounding her home. Find out more about her books at **www.kathidaley.com**

Printed in Great Britain
by Amazon